MANNY'S GIFT

By

Helen Hill

CONTENTS

~ Foreword ~

How many times have we uttered a prayer when we saw no hope, to pass a test in school, to get funds to pay a debt or even to see health restored when the doctors gave up. And it all worked out!

I believe, we all have a road to travel that winds around the hearts and homes of many. Our needs and the needs of others require faith and prayer. And not at our convenience! Prayer needs care... daily, to work.

The residents of Forest Hills are just like you and me. They have problems that need solved. No, it looks like they need miracles! Somebody better be prayed up and on a first name basis with the Miracle Maker.

In fact, it probably would be a good idea for us to stop now and take another 'Good Look at the Good Book.'

Thank God for Pastor Hayden of the Forest Hills Church of Faith ... he seems to have a key to the door of knowledge and a heart of wisdom.

This is just one of his favorite scriptures:

"...be ye doers of the word, and not hearers only, deceiving your own selves.

For if any be a hearer of the word, and not a doer, he is like unto a man beholding his natural face in a glass:

For he beholdeth himself, and straightway forgetteth what manner of man he was.

But whosoever looketh into the perfect law of liberty, and continueth therein, he being not a forgetful hearer, but a doer of the work, this man shall be blessed in his deed." (James 1: 22-25, KJV)

Manny's Gift
Acknowledgments

The first person on my list of acknowledgments is my husband, Danny, who encouraged me all these months while I was preparing my manuscript for publication. He never complained about the late meals and the times I could not spend with him. ('Manny needed me!) "Thank you, Honey, and frozen entrees are no longer on the menu!"

I thank my '*ever-nagging*,' I mean, '*encouraging*' sister, Babe Haskey, who insisted that I keep writing! And my grandson, Andrew Griffith, who helped me do some proofreading while he was visiting. (I think I see a little of Hugh in you!)

There are many wonderful people in my life now who have encouraged, and inspired me in the work of Manny's Gift.

A few years ago, I met a man who was a guiding light for me. I didn't have a lot of self confidence but after one conversation with Morris Williams, I could see possibilities and I could feel my dreams blossom into reality. Not only *could* I write... but I *needed* to write!

And I became aware that others needed to read what I had written! Because of his words of praise, my self esteem has sky rocketed! I may not accomplish everything I want to do in my lifetime, but it will *not* be for the lack of trying. Mr. Williams gave an ample supply of motivation to me. I can only hope someday to do the same for others. Thank you, Mr. Williams!

And I thank all my friends at the First Full Gospel Church as well as Bill Gootee, (the ex-sheriff of Lake City, Florida), and the people at the Hopeful Baptist Church for their help. Bill Gootee helped me with the correct wording for the sheriff's section.

I would like to thank Officer Robert Sepulveda of the Lake City Police Department (and owner of the ATA Martial Arts Academy), for his help with some of the procedural terms.

The following friends have donated their time to read early chapters for me and to reassure me I was making progress! Thanks : Minnie Lee Wallin, Pastor & 'Peaches' Ellis, Linda Larsen, Charles & Edna Johnson, Lloyd & Pat Miller, and Virginia Tiner Nelson. Thanks to Michelle Jones for her photography!

I would also like to thank Melvin and Mary Ann Kirby. I've learned much by their example. They made good models for the pastor's staff in 'Manny's Gift.' Another deacon at my home church, brother Tommie Richardson and his wife, Fran, have always been great encouragers. He calls me "Author." I just hope it's not because he forgot my name! (I didn't forget yours!)

Many of the characters in Manny's Gift reflect traits that I have seen and admired in people I now know or have known. For example, the role models I used for Hugh Hayden is a church deacon and my pastor. Heyward Christie, a deacon, is a big man but gentle and compassionate. My pastor has a shepherd's heart. He loves our church family and he keeps watch over us, protecting and leading us with gospel lights.

Stephen Jones, Michelle's (the photographer's) husband, is an anointed man of God. He is a young minister and his gospel CDs are awesome. But he is also employed at our local Ford dealership. He's not the owner, but Stephen Burdine in chapter 10 has the tenacity that resembles our own Stephen, (who says he likes my book). Thanks for your strength and your integrity, Stephen! It forms a cornerstone for our own house of worship!

Last, but not least, I would like to thank all the Create Space support staff! They were awesome! They kept me on track! No matter how many times I called on them, they were always patient and helpful. I have learned so much from them! And their encouragement picked me up each time I stumbled. They just dusted me off and set my feet back on solid ground where I could see progress and hope again! God bless you all!

Chapter 1 ~ *Angel Wings*

"Code Blue ... room 23... Code Blue... room 23..." The doors shut soundly while the medical personnel rushed through the hallway, the soft soles of their shoes quieting the sounds of emergency response.

The announcement on the public address system made the residents of the hospice center stop for a moment of prayer for the patient in room 23. At times it felt like everyone was a number... 23 obviously was in a fight for his or her life.

Hospice was a compassionate facility for patients nearing the end of life as they knew it. Friendly smiles and encouraging words were two qualities required for working here. No one could ever doubt the effectiveness of those qualities, but let's face it, the end was still very near and one by one, each resident would soon need to be removed, bedding changed and a new face would need to see the smiles and hear all those encouraging words.

Bethany Phillips worked at hospice for two years, believing the place needed her faith and prayers. The pay wasn't terrific but the emotional paycheck arrived with each hug and each hand squeezed as her patients showed their appreciation for her compassion.

Still, each time that white van arrived at the big double doors with those official documented requests from the funeral home, she cringed. She forced back tears and searched for just one more reassuring smile to share with the patients remaining on her duty list.

Through tears, she read the report, room 23... Matilda Baker, age 94, widow, battling lung cancer. As Bethany glanced up at the doctor, his assistant closed the door solemnly on room 23. Matilda was gone.

"Hey, Beth! Can we come out yet?" Bethany

smiled. Manny Jackson was peeking around the door like a mischievous little boy wanting to come outside to play. He was tired of being cooped up in that little room!

"Give me a minute, will you, Manny? Then I'll come in and adjust your IV pole, so you can take a walk. The last time, you just about choked your room-mate with all your wires, remember?" The old man chuckled and said softly, "Take your time, Sweetheart, I'm not planning to go anywhere anytime soon."

Bethany held her clipboard close to her heart, asking God, "Why is he here, Lord? He's such a kind, gentle man. He stayed up with Matilda half the night as she struggled for her breath. He prayed and held her hand, assuring her she would soon be with her Oscar." He said to her, "Do not be afraid! Your Oscar will be excited seeing you coming through heaven's gate!" Matilda smiled and Manny left her to rest.

Why must he meet death struggling with pain and suffering, God? He has so much love to offer and yet in just a few weeks, at best, that big white van will come for ... room 17." Bethany shook her head so she could erase the image from her mind.

She walked past the nurses' station to start open-ing patients' doors, oblivious to the man in the black Armani suit carrying a briefcase. "Excuse me," he said, "I'm looking for Mr. Neimann Jackson. I was told I might find him here."

Bethany stopped and turned to acknowledge the visitor when a sense of *dejevu* took her by surprise. What was it about this man? Why was there such a sense of familiarity? She started to speak to him when he handed her a business card. The card was unique. It said: *Omega Investments, Ltd.* Associate: *Michael Genucci,* Attorney at Law.

"Mr. Neimann Jackson, you said?" She waited for his reply when a voice behind her said, "I believe my name was mentioned. I am Mr. Neimann Jackson, but I haven't heard that name in years. I'm afraid you have me at a disadvantage, young man. I don't know you or why you wish to speak with me."

The businessman turned to look at Manny and stared in disbelief at the old man, his back bent with advanced scoliosis, and his hands trembling. The man he now faced was a small man, aged, withered, and very fragile.

He wore mismatched pajamas and his voice was trembling. But those eyes! There was strength in his eyes that bespoke wisdom from generations gone by. Could this actually be the man he had been seeking all these years?

It hardly seemed possible. The man he had been prepared to meet was, by reputation, a business man, entrepreneur, a man who brought the big corporations to their knees. Neimann Jackson was solely responsible for countless success stories in major cities across the globe!

And yet, Michael stood facing the elderly man, calmly assessing his options. He couldn't just leave... lose this opportunity? Perhaps he had a son. That must be it! His son must be the eccentric giant ... but no ... he would indeed be an elderly man! This *has* to be the end of his search for Neimann Aaron Jackson.

"I'm sorry, sir. My name is Michael Genucci and it would be an honor if you would grant me a few moments of your time. I have some questions I need answered. Maybe you could help me."

Manny nodded, "Moments are precious, son. God only grants us a few and like the dust in the breeze, we move on to eternity." He smiled, lightly touching the young man's shoulder. He said in a formal tone, "Step into my office, son. I may *not* be the man you seek."

Bethany slowly walked to the nurses' station as she glanced over her shoulder at Manny's visitor. She said, "I wonder who he is and what would he want with Manny? Do you think we should just leave them alone? I mean, who knows the scams and the fraud crimes that go on when predators target the elderly?"

Olivia Jefferson, the older black woman at the

desk, smiled, chuckling to Bethany, "I think the only one who might be outfoxed, is our visitor. Our Manny has been looking out for himself for many years now. Didn't you hear all that gibberish: *'like the dust in the breeze, we move on to eternity!'* I mean, have you ever heard such a line in your life?" Olivia laughed hard and her plump body shook uncontrollably.

"Manny's never been known as a philosopher before!" Olivia was getting a boisterous laugh out of his comments, but Bethany considered the words to be true wisdom. Days *are* here and *gone* even before you're ready for it.

She was painfully aware of time passing and the importance of making good choices. She made a few bad choices of her own that she lived to regret. Now, years later, she was still paying the consequences for her actions.

She glanced at the clock on the wall and gasped! "Miss Olivia, would you clock me out? I have *got* to be in my class in twenty minutes. I just can't be late again!"

She waved her hand, never looking up from her work. She shook her head, mumbling, "Mmm... mmm ... mmm! That girl don't know if she's comin' or goin'! Lord, if anyone deserves a break, it's that child right there."

She worked with Bethany for two years. No one worked harder or took her job more seriously than Bethany Phillips. She was a single Mom and Olivia respected her for keeping the child and raising him alone.

The boy's father just walked away, offering no support for the baby. Guess he felt since he told her to have an abortion, his responsibility was over. Thank God she didn't do it. How many babies have to be aborted before our eyes are opened to see we are taking the life of a child? But never once did she complain or ask for help.

Olivia said she wished God would send an angel into Bethany's life to make her life easier. She glanced down at the picture on her desk and as usual, it just warmed her heart. Her daughter, Jasmine, with her husband and three sons smiled back at her... and she counted her blessings again.

Faith played a big part in the changes in her family. It helped to be married to a man who knew how to pray. When Olivia was weak, her husband, John seemed to gain strength. If only Bethany could find a good Christian man who could help ease her heartaches.

But *Olivia's* life was full of heartaches a few years ago. Then God sent an angel into her life to turn it all around. She never saw the angel. But she saw the wings. They were gold, encircling three silver letters ~ NAJ.

Chapter 2 ~ *Olivia's Story*

Jasmine could have been a model. She was so beautiful! When she was born, she took her mama's breath away. At birth, her skin was fair; her olive complexion gave her an exotic appearance. Her thick jet-black hair cascaded in waves resting on her head like an ebony cloud; as a woman, her slender body moved to the rhythm of a secret symphony... she was a vision!

Olivia loved her more than life itself! When she brought her precious baby girl to Pastor Hayden to be dedicated, he held her close and prayed for God's hand to be on her and to guide her throughout her life. He asked God for the gift of wisdom, praying for protection around her.

She and John, Jasmine's father, promised God to raise this baby girl in full accordance with His Word. God knows they did their best. Johnny never called her by her name. He called her his little princess. She seemed to have their kingdom at her beck and call.

Olivia recalled how Jasmine's eyes sparkled when the church brought missionaries from the Philippines to present a program on missions work. Jasmine was seven years old and she volunteered to take up the offering for the missionaries.

There were a few dollar bills given but then Jasmine heard the jingling of loose change. At first, she smiled politely. Then her smile became a frown, as she grew tired of the coins being dropped into the offering plate.

She put her right hand on her hip and scolded, "Now, if *Jesus* was takin' up this offerin', ya'll would be ashamed to put these pidly coins in here. God knows what's in your wallets! He knows what's inside your hearts, too!"

Nervous laughter swept across the sanctuary and

Pastor Hayden rushed to the microphone. He said, "I do believe we have a little missionary in the making, Olivia!" Olivia and John were embarrassed but they laughed with the others. They were proud of Jasmine. They, too, believed she had the makings of a young missionary. She was a child who spoke her mind!

The jingling of the coins was being replaced by all the dollar bills piling up in the offering plate. As Jasmine grinned broadly, she said, "Now *that's* more like it!" The laughter was heard again throughout the congregation, as the little girl moved from row to row. Jasmine took her seat beside her parents. They were proud of their little princess! But that was then ... before Little 'T' came into their neighborhood.

She lost track of all the times she knelt, begging for God to give her young daughter wisdom and bring her back to church. God knows, Olivia did her best. But Jasmine was a young woman with a mind of her own, and an attitude that was untamed.

Her bad choices were reflected in her spiritual immaturity. "Little T" (Tyrell Ivory, III), was one of those very bad choices.

Olivia cringed when she saw how Jasmine was hypnotized by Little 'T'. But Little 'T' owned her... body and soul. She even had his name tattooed across her shoulders below the words, 'Property of:'

Olivia cried for days. He was different from the other boys she dated. Big rings on his hands, his hair worn in dreadlocks, both eyebrows pierced and he convinced Jasmine to join him for her own tattoo. He had his tongue pierced that day, too, but Jasmine declined, thank God!

He had a gang that never left his side. The car he rode in was black with chrome wheels. He had a driver and he rode in the back like a mob boss. His music announced his arrival with the bass pulsating six blocks before he pulled in front of the Jefferson's peaceful home. Olivia was on her knees daily praying to God to get him out of her daughter's life.

The breakup finally came one evening when the

police came to the door asking to speak with Jasmine. On a hot, humid evening in July, police sirens filled the air. It happened that way sometimes. The sizzling' heat of summer brought out the fury and the fire in the souls of evil men! The officers questioned Jasmine about weapons that 'Little T' had in his possession.

Olivia heard her Jasmine's voice answering their question, "He's got no weapons! Just leave 'T' alone!" She could not believe the anger and rage that spewed from her daughter! When had she become so volatile?

The officer, turning to Olivia said, "Sorry to intrude, ma'am, but it's very important that we get our answers from your daughter. Last night we got a 911 call to a drive-by shooting on the eastside. A little three year old girl was killed. This violence has got to stop!"

Jasmine appeared undaunted by the horrendous news of the child's death. She asked him, "Hey! What time was the shooting?" Looking at the report, he said, "It occurred at 2 a.m." Jasmine snarled back, "What's a baby doin' up at 2 a.m. anyhow?"

The officer paused and said slowly, "The child was shot in her bed, and we believe it was 'Little T'... Tyrell... who fired that shot. We found a .38 and if it was, his fingerprints will convict him."

She quickly responded, "No! He couldn't have! Mama, tell him! Little 'T' was with me! He was here all night!" Olivia gasped, "No, Jazz, it's over. Let him go, Sweetheart. He killed a baby girl!"

Jasmine was in tears, "It's not fair, Mama! You never liked 'T'! You are glad he's in trouble!" And the gulf between them grew that night. But 'T' was gone forever. And soon Jasmine left home, vowing to never return.

Olivia mourned for her daughter as if she had died. Fear clutched her heart and she prayed until she was hoarse! Jasmine stayed away for months.

Then in November, she returned, asking her for money. Damien, her new 'man,' was with her and he offered Johnny a beer. Jasmine waited, watching for her father's reaction. But he simply said, "No, thank you, sir, I'm not a drinking man." He picked up a newspaper and walked outside to his favorite chair on the front porch. Olivia, however, never budged. She was angry that alcohol was brought into their home, but she kept silent.

Damien's arm was holding Jasmine close to his side. He leaned down, to whisper something in her ear and she looked uncomfortable. "Mama, I need to talk to you in private," she said. Then she asked if they could give her enough money to pay 'their' rent.

Olivia had to look away and tightly shut her eyes to stop her tears. She prayed that God would take the bitterness out of her heart. 'Lord, speak for me, lest I chase my daughter away with my anger!' She took a deep breath then she spoke to her quietly, "Jazz, I'll always have enough money to take care of you.

But I will not be a party for you to be shackin' up with trash like that. You will always have a home here with your Daddy and me. Come on home, Jazz, where you belong!"

Jasmine turned, full of fury and called to her boy-friend, Damien, "We're leavin'! We are not welcome here in this "holier than thou" home!" And she left Olivia and Johnny, with broken hearts.

"Johnny, was I wrong? What if we lost our baby girl? I just don't know anymore! But I cannot see us paying for that evil man disrespecting our Jasmine! I'm surprised! Can you believe she actually asked us for money to pay for *their* apartment!"

Olivia was angry but her heart was breaking. She loved Jasmine more than life itself. But John just kept rocking. It was almost as if he hadn't heard a word his wife had spoken.

Then he laid down the newspaper and spoke to her. "Livvy, you know what you said to Jasmine was right. And deep down, she knows that you're right. She's just trying to find out where she fits in, in this big old world. She's a good girl, Olivia. We raised her right. But right now, she's making some bad choices.

We need to be strong when she gets weak. She may not even know it yet, but she's counting on us to be making the right choices, even if it makes her angry.

Somewhere deep inside our little girl, she has a plan to return as the Jasmine we've always known she could be. We just have to keep faith in God that He will keep her safe and lead her back home.

Olivia, you need to make peace with the fact that strangers will come into our daughter's life, some good but many that are bad news. I'm sure she will learn to identify the differences and watch for the warning signs that God sends with these strangers."

John reached for his newspaper and paused to say, "I love you, Olivia. You are a good mother. But you worry too much." He laughed and shook his head as he saw her teary smile. How he loved that woman!

John stopped, remembering, "Oh, and speaking of strangers. A man came by this morning. He drove a new car, a Lamborghini, I think! And when he got to the corner, he put it in reverse and parked about twenty feet from where I was working!

I watched him walking towards me and Olivia, his suit shined like silk! And even in December, this man is wearing shades! I never saw one, but it would not surprise me none but that he was a millionaire!

He gave me this card." John took the card from his shirt pocket. "It says, Omega Investments, Ltd. His name is Michael Genucci."

He put the card back in his pocket. Olivia was puzzled. "What's that name again, John?" He took the card out again. "It says, Michael Genucci of Omega Investments, Ltd. Have you ever heard of him?"

Olivia, ignoring his question, asked him, "What did he want?" John shrugged, "He said he's looking for a man named Neimann Jackson. He asked me if I knew where he lived or where he could find him. I never heard of the man and that's what I told him, so he left, but he left me this card in case I thought of anything that could help him."

Olivia stood up and said, "You know, there was

a lawyer who came to Hospice today. It sounds like
the same man to me. But he just wanted to talk to
Manny. I sure hope he's not here to cause that old
man any trouble. They don't come no nicer than our
Manny."

Johnny stood up and put his arm around his
wife. "What do you say we call it a night and let the
rich man, the old man and this tired man give it up
for a well earned sleep?" Olivia kissed him on his
cheek and walked with him to their bedroom, turning
out the lights as they left the room.

The nights no longer brought rest to Olivia. But
each night, in her dreams, she held her baby girl in
her arms, remembering the scent of her bubble gum
kisses. Each night she said goodbye to her daughter ...
again and each time placed her in God's loving care.
So Olivia just waited on God to bring changes to the
life of Jasmine Marie Jefferson, asking nothing for
herself.

The sun was going down behind Backbone Mountain. The gentle man stood gazing at the scenic view
from the third floor of Pleasant Grove Hospital. He
just left John Jefferson's room. After he prayed, John
appeared to be more restful. Now it was time to leave
for there was much work left to do in a short time.

Olivia was arriving just after he left John's room.
"Johnny, can you hear me, Baby?" Olivia wiped away
a tear, and reached to hold his hand. Johnny always
was the love of her life.

Olivia Fields and John Jefferson grew up friends
in Green County, on the banks of Brush Run Creek.
Together, they planned their future. When Olivia was
young, she told John, "You can be a doctor when you
grow up and I'll be your nurse!" (Olivia was always
planning to be a nurse). "And we'll be together all
the time!"

Johnny threw back his head, laughing. "Olivia, I
ain't never gonna be no doctor! I'll probly work in the
coalmines just like all the rest of the Jefferson men.
We work the mines till we can't do it no more, and

you know that!" Olivia shook her head and waited for her chance for rebuttal. "Livvy, you can go and be a nurse and we'll still be together. Of course, you *could* set your sights for a famous doctor with a big house driving a fancy, long car. I can't offer you all that."

Olivia stood to her feet and placed both hands on her hips. "Now see here, *Mr.* John Jefferson! You will *never* step foot in those mines! I'm sick and tired of goin' to funerals, hearin' their women cry 'cause their man was trapped in those tombs! I don't care if you pump gas at the old Sinclair station for the next forty years, but you ain't workin' them mines. You got that? And I ain't marryin' nobody else but you! And we do *not* need to ever talk about it again... so you get that straight, *Mr.* Jefferson!" John laughed hard and hugged her, holding her close.

"Yes, ma'am! I am yours forever!" But Olivia wondered how long forever would be when the highway patrol called her last night. He lost control of his pickup as he drove down Horseshoe Bend. No one saw how it happened but his red pickup was spotted by a passing motorist and an ambulance brought him to the emergency room.

The attending physician told her they called in a surgeon to operate on his ruptured spleen but now, his kidneys were failing. His only hope was for a new kidney. But the donor list was very long and John's condition was too critical! He needed a miracle to live!

Olivia bowed her head as she prayed for God's mercy, "Dear God, please don't take my Johnny. He's all I got, Lord! Even Jasmine has left us. Please, God spare his life!" The door to his room opened slowly, without a sound, as the pastor entered. He laid his hand on Olivia's shoulder.

"Olivia, are you and Johnny up for a visitor?" As she turned, she saw Jasmine standing beside the pastor. "My beautiful baby girl!" Jasmine was still a vision to behold! She was smiling but her eyes were full of tears and her face was swollen... from tears? Bruises on her face appeared to be healing.

Olivia's heart went out to Jasmine; her heart was breaking as she felt her daughter's pain. She saw the scars and imagined the battered life she endured.

"Mama?" She reached for her mother's hand cautiously. She wasn't sure whether she could accept her back in her life... or if she had the right to ask.

She left her parents' home and vowed she would never return. First, she had turned to Little 'T' and his life of crime, drugs and violence. Then her next bad choice took her into an abusive relationship with Damien.

Last week, she finally left him. But she carried several reminders of his abusive nature. Her left eye had been black and swollen shut. Her face had cuts from his fist and her ribs were bruised, and some bones were even broken.

How could she be so off track? All she wanted was a love like her parents shared. Instead, she was attracted to the night life and power that came with Little 'T.' An abusive world pulled her into the night and left it's scars on her until she had to crawl back like the prodigal son. Now she waited nervously for Olivia's response.

"Jazz, I have prayed for so long for your return. Please don't say you will come back to me and give me hope only to lose you again. Your father... *I*... am just not strong enough to say goodbye again!" Olivia dropped into the chair by John's bed, sobbing with a broken heart, as only a mother could, when her child was lost.

Jasmine went to her mother's side and hugged her. "No, Mama, I'm not going anywhere. I'll be here for you and Daddy for as long as it takes to get him back on his feet!" Olivia clutched Jasmine close to her and cried. Together they laughed and bathed in the release of their burden, drinking in sweet moments of answered prayer.

Pastor Hayden watched while the women enjoyed their reunion with tears and laughter. He smiled and praised God for the return of their lost child. "Olivia,

I hate to interrupt this beautiful reunion, but John's doctor needs you to make a list of possible compatible donors ... in case, well, it's really just procedure."

Jasmine stood up and said, "Me! It's me! I am probably compatible, Mama, I'll do it!" Olivia shook her head, "No, Child, I can't let you do that! I just got you back. I just can't take that chance. Something might go wrong and I could lose both of you! I'll do it myself! If I lost Johnny, I wouldn't want to live, anyways! I'll give my kidney to John and that's final."

The doctor arrived just as Jasmine volunteered to be the donor. "Jasmine, I was hoping you would be here. Your Daddy really needs you now. And no, you *can't* be the donor, Olivia, and *that's* final! Your blood pressure and your weak heart are just two factors that disqualify you from being a donor. But now *you*, Jasmine, if *you* want to be tested, then you need to come with me,quickly. The surgeon will be in soon to talk with you, Olivia."

Jasmine touched her mother's worried face and said, "It'll be okay, Mama, you'll see. Daddy needs me so I'll be back right after the test. Everything is going to be fine, Mama. You'll see. I love you!"

Johnny was moving and wincing in pain. It was hard for Olivia to watch. She grabbed a damp cloth and gently wiped his face, as he struggled to speak to her. But he was determined to make his wife understand his request. "Olivia." He gasped, trying to get the strength to speak, "Please listen to me. You can't do this, Baby. We can't do this... tell them I won't have the surgery. We got no health insurance... and we got no money to pay for it!"

Olivia began to cry. "Johnny, you still need this operation! Without it, you will die! I ain't ready to be no widow so you *are* going to have this surgery! Do you hear me, *Mr.* John Jefferson?" Tears were streaming down her face.

John's eyes were brimming. He said, "Baby, I'm sorry. I should have worked harder. If I was a better provider... you..." His voice broke as his pain worsened.

-14-

"Livvy, we can't pay for this. You could lose everything and I still might not make it. Do *not* sacrifice everything for a *chance* I might recover. Baby, please, don't risk it for me."

Hugh Hayden, standing in the hallway came in to comfort him. "Hey, Johnny, you don't need to be concerned! You're one of the family! You know we won't let you down. God wants His children to look out for one another so you just let the doctor do what *he* has to do to get you on the mend. God will take care of you *and* your family so let Olivia sign those forms and quit worrying. God is in control."

Johnny closed his eyes and Hugh prayed that His mercy would be present to bring Johnny peace so he could make wise choices.

Olivia was reassuring John when she heard the man approaching John's room. She didn't want to tell John, but that doctor looked like a college boy. He was not old enough to have much experience, she was sure of that. When he saw Olivia Jefferson standing in the doorway, he smiled broadly, looking even younger.

"Well, it looks like we have a winner! Jasmine is the perfect match for her daddy and I have already booked the celebrity suite just for Mr. John Jefferson." The young surgeon was confident and ready to do the transplant.

"I'm sorry, guys, I'm getting ahead of myself, so please, allow me to introduce myself. My name is Paul Samson Santos and I am the Chief of Surgery at the Mercy Hospital.

I suppose I have been chosen to do your transplant because I have done this more times than I can count. That means, I'm pretty good at it. I'll try to answer any questions you might have. We really need to make this quick, though, because his kidneys are really ready for showtime, okay?"

Jasmine entered the room wide-eyed, and asked, "*Samson*? Is your name *really* Paul *Samson* Santos? Really?" He stopped, staring at Jasmine for a second and spoke gently, "Yes, ma'am, it really is. My parents were missionaries in the Philippines when I was born. They named me Samson because he learned that with God, all of his battles would be victories. And besides, I wasn't old enough to vote on their choice of names.

But one interesting fact is that my family came to the Forest Hills Church of Faith years ago and we presented our mission work. Of course, that was years ago, and I was just nine years old. That's when I met your pastor."

He looked again at Jasmine. He couldn't take his eyes off her, who returned his gaze with pleasure. He pulled his stare away long enough to ask, "Any other questions for me?"

Olivia was reluctant to mention the costs, "Sir, we don't have any insurance. And I know we should, but we can't afford it now." She paused, "But that don't mean you won't get paid," she said hurriedly, "No, sir, the Jeffersons always pay their debts. But I can't say how long..."

He raised his hand. "Whoa!" He shook his head. "Someday I know I'll learn to get the cart behind the horse. I am sorry, I really am. He held up a familiar envelope and Hugh Hayden gasped when he saw it. The gold wings encircled the silver letters NAJ. "Your medical costs have been paid in full. In fact, your benefactor arranged for your transplant to be done by yours truly. So relax. God is in control. You already got a couple of miracles and I don't believe He's done yet." He reached for John's hand as he asked, "Are you ready, sir?" John smiled and nodded, "Let's get it done, son."

The bedside rails were locked in position. Olivia gave him one last kiss as the nurses came to prepare him for his transplant.

She paced nervously in the hallway waiting for John to be brought back to his hospital room. After all, he was not a young man, but he never had any major health issues; at least none Olivia knew about. He was never one to complain if he was sick. He was convinced that a little hard work was probably the good Lord's cure for many common ailments.

If there had not been an accident last week that sent John Jefferson to the hospital by ambulance, they would probably never know anything about his kidney disease.

He needed a transplant to save his life and his daughter was a perfect match for donating. Jasmine was already out of surgery and doing well in recovery so Olivia was waiting to hear the news of Johnny's condition.

She was praying for God's hand of mercy on the Jefferson family. 'Please, Lord, let that young man be right when he said You were not done giving out miracles.'

She stopped pacing and turned when she heard a man call out to her. "Mrs. Jefferson! Excuse me, ma'am, but may I have a word with you?" Dr. Paul Santos walked toward her, still dressed in his scrubs. He was holding a patient's file in his right hand. Olivia rushed to meet him. 'Oh, Lord, please don't let this be bad.' Instantly, he recognized the look of fear on Olivia's face. He stopped dead in his tracks!

"Oh, no! I just did it again, didn't I? I am *so* sorry. I did *not* mean to scare the life out of you! He is doing great. In fact, they wheeled him into recovery as I got off the elevator. Just give them a minute to finish up in there and then you can see him." She shook his hand, "Thank you, Doctor! I can't never thank you enough! Oh, dear Jesus, I thank You for sparing my Johnny!" Olivia was crying tears of joy. Dr. Santos put his arm around her. She looked up and said, "You wanted to have a word with me? Was there a problem? You said everything went well with his surgery, right?"

The young surgeon smiled sheepishly and said, "Everything is great. I finished in the O.R. And then something stuck in my mind! I think you may be able to help me solve a mystery." This time Olivia took charge and said, "Come over here. Let's sit and talk for a spell, ok?"

Everything was going to be fine now! Johnny was recovering, Jasmine was back, and God sent an angel to pay the hospital bill. "What can I help you with, Dr. Santos?" The man smiled, saying, "Well, for starters, you can stop calling me 'Doctor.' My name is Paul and I intend to marry your daughter."

Olivia's jaw dropped! She was speechless! Paul laughed before explaining, "I told you that my parents came to your church as missionaries years ago. I was just a little boy. Jasmine was the pretty little girl who took up the offering for our ministry, right?

I'll never forget the way she stood up there in church and *demanded* that they rethink their offering." He and Olivia shared the memory and laughed as they remembered that service so many years ago.

Paul said, "I told my parents that night that I would marry her someday. Mother said, 'Well, Son, if it is God's will, you will cross paths again.' I knew there was something familiar about Jasmine when I met your family before we did the donor test on her. But she never left my mind."

Olivia touched his hand and asked, "And you say you want to marry my little girl?" He said, "I do. Oh, I suppose we have to get a preacher before I say my 'I do's'!" He laughed and Olivia joined in.

The next few months were busy while Johnny was healing. Jasmine stayed by her daddy's side while her mother returned to work at Hospice. Paul Santos was *very* busy trying to tell Jasmine they were a match made in heaven. The smile never left Olivia's face as she saw Jasmine being courted and pampered by a loving Christian man.

Pastor Hayden told them to enjoy these months of awareness and friendship to test their feelings. Of course, Paul was busy making plans for a honeymoon before Jasmine even accepted his proposal. He hadn't learned that the horse before the cart works best. But the Jefferson family learned to love Paul just the way he was. It was a joy to hear Jasmine's laugh again. Her past was gone and her future was just beginning.

Their pastor counseled them for ten weeks after Jasmine came to the altar and renewed her commitment to God. (Hugh counseled all engaged couples before a wedding). So Paul *'Samson'* Santos and Jasmine Marie Jefferson were united in holy matrimony.

They spent their honeymoon in the Philippines. Paul's parents proudly welcomed Jasmine into their family. Ten months later, they became the proud parents of triplets! There were three sons. Paul suggested the names 'Shadrach, Meshach, and Abednego!' But Jasmine overruled and her boys were named, Paul, John, and Mark. Paul, of course, for daddy, and John, for Jasmine's daddy, and Mark, for Paul's daddy.

Daddy Paul said their names were just a little boring. But everyone agreed that *nothing* would ever be boring in that family!

Who would have known that Paul loved Jasmine all those years so long ago? How would anyone have known that he had become a gifted surgeon? Who had the ability to know that Jasmine would be needed as a kidney donor for her father? And Who found her just in time? Olivia pondered on this often.

It had to be the same one who sent that special letter to Paul, paid the price to save John Jefferson's life and brought blessings to a Christian family, who loved the Lord with all their heart.

Undoubtedly, it had to be the hand of God, that opened all the windows of heaven and poured out a blessing.

Now, Olivia had just two words to say, "Praise God!" Only the Spirit of God could have sent the envelope with the golden wings encircling silver letters, NAJ.

Chapter 3 ~ *Bethany's Story*

Olivia watched through the bay windows in the dayroom as Bethany dashed to her car in the parking lot, praying traffic would be kind to her. The college was just five miles away but it took careful timing to get a parking space close enough to her classroom and still sign in to class on schedule.

Mr. Pearson, the instructor, warned the class on the first day, "If you want to get on my bad side, try coming to class late. My time is valuable and it is no less than disrespect to think I should wait for *your* arrival to begin the class. I will not tolerate it."

Bethany was late twice already and she felt his cold wrath. *'Please, Lord, put wings on my feet so I won't be late...'* She wanted to get her nursing degree and was determined that nothing would stand in her way!

If she would have made the right decisions years ago, she would be an RN by now. But there was a little thing called love that side tracked her for many years. How could she have been so blind? Has it really been that long? Why, it seemed like just yesterday she was in homeroom class drawing hearts with initials, B.P. loves M.B., and of course TLF, (true love forever). Well, *that* forever sure didn't last very long.

M.B., Matt Bosley was student body president, valedictorian, the boy most likely to succeed. When he finally noticed Bethany, she had almost given up hope. She had a crush on him since her freshman year, but he was much too popular to date a quiet little nobody like her. He was the captain of the football team!

It seemed like all the fun things in school, like pep rallies and football games, even prom night was competing with her church schedule. Mama was *not* going to let socializing be her ticket to hell! Mama was a 'born again, Bible totin' child of the King!'

Daddy loved Mama like crazy but he knew all

about her faith and convictions first hand. He was not a church goer but before he died, he repented and became a firm believer in Jesus Christ. He was humble and quiet, but you knew when Daddy talked about Jesus, he was talking about a love for his savior. And Mama was praising God, crying tears of joy when Daddy got saved.

They were a crazy couple, in love with Jesus and with each other. That was the love Bethany was seeking. And Matt Bosley caused her heart to flutter, flop and he turned her world upside down.

Daddy was dying of pancreatic cancer and yet he never complained. He greeted her each day with a big smile, expecting to pull her close like he always did when she was his 'little peep.' But every day, despite their prayers for his healing, he got steadily worse. He knew about Matt; he told her to be very careful.

Matt was not a Christian so Bethany used the argument that Mama was the Christian first in their home and eventually Daddy received salvation. Surely God had such a plan for Matt to get saved.

Could it be that this was just the formula for the Phillips women? Sadly, Daddy shook his head, "Is that what God says? You know His word better than I. So tell me, Little Peep, what His word tells you."

And yes, Bethany *did* know all the stories, like a house divided, and two being unequally yoked ... she knew He had a plan for her life that did not include her marrying a sinner to pull her away from church.

"Besides, your mother would never stand for it." He laughed as he visualized Mary being asked to bless the engagement of her beautiful only child to Matthew Bosley, an arrogant, self-centered young man who saw no future for himself in 'organized religion.'

He knew Matt was intelligent and determined to be a successful attorney. His ambition was to go into politics. But none of Matt's attributes would appease his wife, Mary. She only agreed to allow Bethany to socialize with him in hopes of getting him 'in through the church doors.'

Matt had plenty of admirers, but Bethany still dreamed of the day when her pastor, Hugh Hayden, would ask him those thrilling words, "Matthew Bosley, do you take Bethany Phillips to be your lawful wife?" Maybe her dream would come true someday. But for now, it was enough that he smiled at her with that crooked smile that melted her heart.

He possessively held her close by his side when they walked together at school and everyone knew she was 'Matt's girl.' She felt honored that he had chosen her out of all those girls who were crazy about him! They were apparently, 'made for each other,' but there was one problem that still remained.

He saw 'their problem' as a *'temporary'* doubt, a *'little '* lack of trust. She saw it as sinful temptation. Bethany was determined to 'save herself' for her husband on their wedding night. This was to be the anticipation of all the preparations, pure and holy!

Mama always told her if a young man truly loved her, he would never expect her to devalue herself with premarital sex. That was the final treasure a virgin could offer to her new husband. And if a man persisted, it was a dead giveaway that she was not his true love, but just a mindless toy.

But in all fairness, she thought Matt could never be expected to fully understand her convictions, since he was not raised with the same values the Phillips household held dear. With such conflict going on in Bethany's heart, it was inevitable that a collision of compromise was due to erupt; and it did the night of the Sweetheart Prom, 2001.

The school rented the Arts Pavilion Center for the senior prom. The theme was "Beyond Possibilities" and it was spectacular! It was the first year the prom was held in February, on Valentine's Day, a day for lovers.

The ceiling was designed to recreate the illusion of the universe. A sparkling strobe light gave images of stars and planets created by halogen effects to lift the imagination. There was a sense of Creation and life with the deep blues of the oceans and rich, midnight

-22-

blues for the night.

Indeed, anything truly seemed possible that night. As Matt pulled her close for the last dance, she lost the will to resist. Together, they walked hand in hand into the night. As they entered the parking lot, he pulled her into his arms and kissed her slowly... sensually. He opened her door but his eyes were locked on her soul.

She tried to breathe in the fragrance of the viburnum blossoms but she was intoxicated by the scent of the man who had lured her away. It was a mystical, physical high ... every inch of her body kept yearning for more... for a while.

Then all the decorations were ripped down, the halogen lights were taken back to the rental store and Matt became indifferent. She no longer was the future, the promise of anticipation. Now she was just his past, used and then tossed aside. He lost his desire for her. The challenge was gone and Bethany was brokenhearted... and ashamed.

She believed in a promise of forever love, being a soul mate for life. He had said, 'Nothing could ever change the way he felt for her. His love was only able to grow. This was a journey he intended to walk with her hand in hand for the rest of their lives.' Sweet words!

Yes, Matt had the real makings of a politician; he made promises to get the results he wanted, but now Bethany saw a new image in *her* mirror and she wasn't very proud of what she saw.

She had surrendered to the enemy and now she was abandoned. How could she ever tell her mother? Oh, Daddy would hold her close, but his heart would break for her!

"God, what have I done? Forgive me, Lord, for I have sinned against Your word. Let me once more feel Your presence. So speak to me and comfort me, Holy Spirit, for I feel lost. I know that You love me unconditionally. You will *never* walk away from me. You will not forsake me no matter what road I take in life.

Bring me back to your pathway. I need to be held
once more in Your wondrous love, Jesus!"

Bethany accepted the Lord's forgiveness but she
knew there would still be days of sadness and fear, a
sense of betrayal and the painful loneliness within her
spirit.

Matt shattered her innocence. He robbed her of
her dreams and her expectations. Now what could she
offer the man with whom she would someday choose
to share her life? How could she ever trust herself to
love again?

As Bethany quietly slipped into her seat in class,
Mr. Pearson was facing the window across the room.
"So nice of you to join us today, Ms. Phillips. I hope
I haven't inconvenienced you too much, expecting you
to be on time for my class?" A light ripple of laughter
moved through the classroom. Her friend, Ashley, gave
her a reassuring hug and a smile. Could anything else
go wrong?

Reliving the old 'sentimental journey' served no
purpose, yet Bethany could not avoid it. How could
she? Every time she held her son, Jacob, Matt's child,
she relived that prom night. She knew for sure, she
did the right thing when she refused to have the abortion that Matt offered to pay for.

How could he not see the gift of a precious life
given to them from God? Their son was perfect! But
Matt refused to even claim his child. He never gave
her support of any kind. In fact, he just walked out
of their lives. If Matt didn't want his son, Bethany
decided to love him twice as much. She would work
twice as hard, if necessary, to give him the life that
he deserved, even without a father. He would never
be a burden for her.

"Ms. Phillips, are you here to participate in the
class or to just take up space on that seat? If it's not
too much to ask, do you think you could read and
answer the next question?" Bethany stammered, "Uh,
did you say ... the next question?" Bethany knew she
answered him weakly. "I'm sorry, sir, but could you

tell me what number you're on?"

The laughter brought humiliation, and she was embarrassed to be caught daydreaming. Sometimes, her job at Hospice, taking care of her son, studying, and taking college classes at night all became a rotating sphere of confusion and fatigue.

What she needed was a day off to do nothing but rest, which seemed impossible. She held back the incredible urge to laugh out loud. She dropped her head to gain control of her sanity. They would think she was crazy if she started laughing now for no apparent reason!

Bethany slowly came to the conclusion that she was at her wit's end, nearing exhaustion, causing her erratic behavior. But one thing was certain, something just had to give or she would be sure to break!

'Lord, You said You will never put more on us than we can bear, but I don't know how much more I can take! I really need Your help.' Bethany knew her mother would *gladly* step up and take over the job of caring for Jacob. But Jacob was *her* baby boy... *her* responsibility!

She provided for him for the last ten years now and loved every minute of their life together. But with all her effort and sacrifice, surely she should be seeing the proverbial 'light at the end of the tunnel.' Instead, there was always another dark cloud, a debt, draining all hope from her finances.

She never lost the shame of giving away her self respect, throwing away the treasure of her innocence, her virginity, to a man like Matt. She disappointed her parents. Bethany saw it in her mother's eyes when she told her she was having Matt's baby.

Little Jacob was born the Friday before Thanksgiving, 2001. Bethany's father died just weeks before. If he could have just held on to life long enough to meet his grandson!

Pancreatic cancer took his life with no apology. She knew his death was merciful. He suffered for years but Bethany and her mother continued to pray for him. The memory of her father's death came flooding her heart as she recalled his last days.

Mary Phillips was an independent woman and nothing could shake her faith. And heaven help anyone who tried to change her mind! Thomas could sit for hours and just watch Mary read her Bible and pray. He loved everything about her. He laughed when she said one day he would get saved.

Without a doubt, Thomas believed she was able to pray down snowflakes into Hades! He was a little fearful that he would disappoint her if he got saved and received a lesser portion of the zeal that Mary received with her own salvation.

As he sat there one day, he was thinking about Mary, and the thought 'came' to him, "What if you *did get Mary's portion?* Could you handle it?" It was like a voice from heaven.

Thomas told Bethany he started laughing and he couldn't seem to stop! He pictured himself like an old marionette, jumping insanely out of control. The idea was hilarious. Bethany laughed when he told the story to her. Bethany said, "What did you do then, Daddy?"

He composed himself and smiled. Bashfully, he said, "I went on ahead and got saved anyways." She jumped up and said, "What did you say!?" She could not wait to hear the rest of the story. "Well, after the Lord and I enjoyed our private little joke, He said to me, 'Don't worry, Thomas. I have just the plan for *your* salvation and I can guarantee you it will be right for you. You will love it.' And I surely do!"

Bethany wanted to know more! She stood before her father, Thomas, and saw the glow he had and was amazed. Mama's and Daddy's personalities were very different and God satisfied both with His wisdom. But Mama was never going to see Daddy healthy and healed no matter how much she fasted and prayed.

Someday, Bethany wanted to ask God, "Why?" Why there was cancer and pain? Since God was the Great Physician, why didn't He just heal everyone and take away all the suffering of His children?

When Thomas Phillips died, Pastor Hayden spoke at the bereavement service. He began Thomas' eulogy by praising the man for his strength and his devotion to God and family. Bethany never asked the pastor directly why God let cancer claim the lives of so many loved ones. But somehow he answered her unspoken question in a way that she would never forget.

He said, "In our minds, we often question God. Maybe He made a mistake! He overlooked our needs! He took away our husband, (or our father, brother, or child) and we weren't ready to let him go!" The minister paused, and said, "Are we *ever* ready to let go?"

The congregation was silent as they considered his question. "How glorious it would be if our God would hear *this* cry from our selfish hearts: 'We want to *live* in these old earthly bodies forever; No pain, no more sickness! Please God! *If You love me, You will do it!* (I know we have all heard someone use *that* line before)." Some nodded and smiled. Hugh paused and he turned aside.

"But I heard Ms. Olivia tell her class something a few weeks ago. A young lad had planned a practical joke. He placed a wet sponge on her chair. He was just waiting for her to take her soggy seat. But she looked across the classroom and without even glancing back at her chair, she said, "It ain't happenin', child!"

He waited for the gentle laughter to subside and said softly, "And so I quote Ms. Olivia today, with all the love and compassion I have, 'It ain't happenin', child."

But take comfort in the message He sent to us long, long ago. Simply this: 'For God so loved the world, He gave His only begotten Son, that *whosoever* ... (that's you and me), believeth on Him should not perish but have everlasting life.' That one sentence puts all things in order. God loves us and He's *still* in control. Now let us pray."

Bethany felt peace settle upon her. She vowed to keep her dad's memory alive if only in stories. When her baby was born on November 22ⁿᵈ, she *knew* there

-27-

would be stories she would share about his Grandpa. He was a great man ... and she named her baby Jacob Thomas. Little Jacob, she decided, will make him very proud!

Mary Phillips laid her husband to rest. Many of her friends and family were surrounding her. Bethany stayed until her baby delivered. But it was hard for Mary to step aside and allow Bethany to be Jacob's mommy. So when Eloise, Mary's older sister, asked if she would want to come to California for a visit, the invitation was accepted.

It was the hardest decision she ever made. There was the controlling Mary who was convinced that her daughter needed her for all her years of experience. Then there was the side of Mary that knew if she did stay, she could do irreparable damage to their relationship. So she left (as Bethany advised).

But more than once Bethany cried, hoping she made the right choice by sending her away. Mary left her daughter with a lingering love and prayers from a mother's heart. They both knew there was more than enough to suffice.

She felt Mr. Pearson's presence overshadow her daydreaming, and she was startled when he spoke to get her attention, "The *rest* of us are on page 204, the procedures' paragraph. Would you be so kind as to read and answer question #7? Oh, and thank you for your class participation."

Mr. Pearson knew he was being hard on her. He knew Bethany's story. 'She was a struggling, single mother' and sometimes he felt guilty when he berated her. But he just knew he had to push her and keep her mad enough to get through his class. He was so determined that his star pupil would succeed!

He saw the fire in her eyes when he told her she may not be cut out to be a nurse. Then he also reminded her that Wal-Mart was hiring cashiers. "But of course," he added snidely, "I don't believe even Wal-Mart would employ you at *your* convenience."

As he turned to walk away, he rapped his ruler

on the edge of her desk with one loud, cracking tap! No one would have given his gesture a second thought, but Bethany glanced up at the sound and broke down in tears.

George was not prepared for her reaction. He apologized and tried to calm her down. "Ms. Phillips? Bethany, are you okay? I'm sorry if I upset you. Uh, Ashley, would you escort Ms. Phillips to the ladies' room, please?"

As Bethany rose from her seat, she covered her face and wiped her eyes, trying to compose herself; she knew she couldn't miss this class. "I'll be fine. I am so sorry! It has just been a really bad day."

Mr. Pearson looked at her with compassion and said, "We all have days like that. Why don't you go on home early and get some rest? It'll be all right. You can make up your work." Bethany nodded in agreement.

She wanted to go quickly; all eyes were on her! What would she say to Jake when she came home early? She wasn't feeling well? Well, she really wasn't feeling well at all. She just couldn't deal with any more stress in her life, but she did not want Jake to hear it from her. She drove home, determined to find a smile for her son before she reached the front door.

"Hey, Mom! Whatcha' doin' home so early? It's not even dark yet!" Usually she arrived home just in time to hear Jacob's prayers and get reassured that he finished his homework, took his bath and brushed his teeth. Would she ever have time to share a life with her son?

"I didn't want to miss out on the game tonight. You said it would be awesome, remember?" He eyed her suspiciously, "Yeah, right, you don't even like football!" She laughed at his sarcasm and touseled his hair. "No, I don't, but I *love you*!" He dropped to the floor in a fit of giggles. How could she live one day without this joy in her life?

She thanked God for him. Suddenly, he excitedly jumped to his feet, "Hey, Mom! You gotta see this really cool letter that came today! There's gold wings in the corner and three silver letters that say, NAJ. Even the envelope feels funny! Look at it!"

He picked up the letter from her desk and gave it to her, anxious to hear about the contents. He did not exaggerate a bit. The envelope felt textured like paper currency. She carefully opened the letter, taking notice of the gold wings and silver letters that shined and reflected the light. Even the letterhead was hand-written in beautiful calligraphy, as though created by some ancient scribe.

She read the message slowly, carefully absorbing the details one by one. She searched for a postmark or return address, but only the gold wings and silver letters filled the box for the return address.

Then she realized, there was no postage affixed, either. Which meant the letter was hand delivered. But by whom? "Jacob, where did this letter come from? I know it didn't come through the mail."

Jake was in the kitchen, looking for something to eat, hungry as usual. He leaned into the doorway and spoke with a mouthful of potato chips, "I dunno. Mrs. Dunn, next door, said some old man gave it to her. He said to be sure that you... I think she said, the daughter of Thomas Phillips,' was the tented 'cipient or something like that. Anyways, she said I had to make real sure you got it."

Bethany stared at the odd letter and said quietly, "Oh, my! Now what do I do with this?" She decided to call her pastor. He told her when her mother, Mary went to California he would be close by if she needed anything. She was sure this qualified as a need.

Pastor Hayden was surprised to get a call from Bethany Phillips. But he was *not* surprised about the letter. "Pastor, could you come to my place? Jake and I got a letter today and... well, I would just feel better if you could take a look at it. I'd like your advice." He knew another letter had surfaced, but he still had nothing but questions.

The entire letter was written in beautiful script.

-30-

The body of the letter related the story of Elijah:

'He trusted God to lead him to water when he was thirsty; the ravens brought him meat to nourish him. After he learned to trust God, he was sent to Zarepheth to a widow and her son who was preparing to die from starvation. A drought left them with few provisions. The prophet instructed her to trust God, who told her to feed the prophet first. And then she and her son would never do without. This was a simple plan: 1. Don't worry 2. Do your best 3. Trust God to provide the rest.' Such beautiful Words to live by from an unchanging God!'

"Pastor, there are *official* legal documents in here, too. The first is a trust fund for Jake! And here is a deed to a home in Rose Court. Why would someone give these gifts to Jake? Is it a mistake or is it a bad joke?!" The Pastor shook his head, "No, Bethany, it's no mistake and I can almost guarantee you now that it's all legitimate. But where it came from, I have no clue." Bethany was shocked. "How can it be? Why?"

The minister relaxed on the sofa and said, "Beth, ya got any coffee? This will take a while." Jake ran to the kitchen saying, "I got it! Stay there, Mom, and don't anyone say another word 'til I get back!"

It never occurred to her not to include Jake in this meeting. She had a special relationship with Jake and besides, after he was given the letter, she couldn't keep any of the details from him even if she tried!

Pastor Hayden said, "I have an idea where this got started. But I don't have the full story, at least not yet. If memory serves me right, your dad told me that several patients were being encouraged to cherish the moments of every day.

One question posed to the patients was, 'What was the happiest moment of your life thus far? Then the second question was, what is the one regret you have in your life besides your cancer diagnosis? And the third, if you had a magic lamp, besides a cure for your disease, what would your wish be?'

-31-

Thomas said his happiest moment by far, was holding his newborn daughter. His greatest regret was not being around to help her raise *her* baby. When it came to the third question, he just excused himself as he walked away from the group. He 'never believed in *magic*,' he said with a smile."

The pastor reached over and squeezed Bethany's hand when she brushed away a tear, smiling. "Yes, I can hear Daddy saying that, all right. He'd never be confrontational; he'd just walk away, refusing to hear any of it."

Bethany chuckled, "Now, my *Mama* would have rolled up her sleeves and prepared for the battle." She turned to the pastor, and said, "I appreciate you coming out and sharing this with me! I really miss him." She rose from the sofa but he stopped her.

"Wait, Beth, there's more... when Thomas stepped out to get a breath of fresh air, he sat on the porch, on the front side of the clinic. One of the nurses, (I think her name was Corene), came out to check on him.

A patient was curled up in the chair next to him in pain. Your dad was praying quietly for him so he didn't hear his name called by the nurse. She touched his shoulder and said, 'Mr. Phillips, your treatment room is now available. You'll feel much better after you see the doctor, Hon.'

But your father looked at the other man, curled up in the fetal position, in pain, and said, 'Take him, I'll just wait.' Corene whispered to him that the man was waiting for the van to pick him up. He came in hoping to see the doctor but no appointments were available. He just had to wait to see the doctor the following day.

If your dad offered his own appointment to him, he would be giving up *his* treatment for the day. He looked back to the man who apparently retreated to a deep sleep to escape his pain. Thomas said, 'Then you must take him. Give him some relief from *his* pain.'

Corene started to object but your father was very

persistent; the staff wheeled the other man into the treatment room. He smiled his thanks weakly as they took him inside. Thomas stayed on the porch. Then, out of nowhere, came an elderly man and sat down next to him. He asked Thomas why he gave up his treatment. He told him, God would ease his pain enough for now.

The old man nodded. He said, 'And what *would* your one wish be if *God* would grant it and magic wasn't in the equation?' He eyes filled with tears as he told me his answer. 'I would want a life for my Little Peep, where she could be safe and secure, a real future for her and the baby.' Thomas said he sat back with his eyes shut to hold back his tears. But when he opened his eyes again, the old man was gone.

He started to doubt his own sanity. He asked me if I thought he dreamed up the old man story. I said I didn't know if he had or not. But I told him that stranger things than that have been known to happen.

But now this letter appears to be the result of your father's and the old man's conversation at the treatment center! If you'd like, I will have it checked out for you. But I have to say though, I can't think of anyone more deserving of such a blessing!"

The Commerce Bank told Bethany the documents were ready to be signed. A trust fund had been set up for Jacob. His education would not be a concern for her anymore. There would be enough funds available for any school he chose to attend, and more besides.

The house in Rose Court was like a doll house. Each room was beautifully furnished. Bethany kept pinching herself making sure it was not a dream. Now she and Jake could leave that tiny apartment. Both of them would have their own private bathroom! She was like a child at Christmas as she walked through her new home.

But she was not without questions, just answers. She looked out the window heavenward to thank God one more time, for her son's future, their new home, and NAJ, whoever he was.

Chapter 4 ~ *The Pearson Family*

Part 1 *Alan & Natalie Pearson's Story*

George Pearson excused Bethany from evening classes. She was obviously distraught and needed some time for herself. He asked Ashley to see that she got home safely. His action surprised some of the class, this revelation that Pearson actually had a heart!

He knew someone once said he was as 'cold as a stone' but that wasn't always the case. But he *was* always a perfectionist. Years ago, he overheard some one in the teacher's lounge describe him as being a classic case of OCD, (Obsessive, Compulsive, Disorder).

Much of his character traits were inherited from his father, Alan Glenn Pearson, an attorney in private practice who headed up his own law firm. He hired several law clerks and had four associates that were under him.

He was a successful lawyer, with an eye for detail. Some in his firm mocked him just for laughs. They said, "Son, you make sure you cross all your t's and you dot all your I's or you'll lose your case *and* your credibility!" They laughed but it was those traits that made the practice owned by Alan Pearson, Attorney At Law the successful firm it had become!

Alan had an orderly life. He mapped out all the details and followed his plan to the letter, including his marriage. Miss Natalie Ruth Jones and Mr. Alan Glenn Pearson were married in June, 1972, in the Forest Hills Church of Faith.

The church was beautifully decorated in red roses and baby's breath and the bride wore a long white gown. The reception was held in the Community Hall and rice bouquets were handed out to all the well wishers. The sun was shining brightly as they left for their honeymoon in the Bahamas.

Everything was going well, just as he planned for in their perfect world. Alan graduated from law school and passed the bar exam two years before. He and another attorney went into private practice. His life was on schedule. He was a perfectionist who had a plan for everything and his clients loved him.

Natalie quit her office job at Forest Hills Realty to become a full time wife and hopefully, mother. Alan purchased their two-story home within the first six months of their wedding; Natalie was thrilled with the choices he made. He also chose the furniture, a new BMW for Natalie and a Cadillac for himself. He was indeed a successful man.

His wife was never consulted for decisions. He told her once he was the man of the house and she was the homemaker. It worked out nicely for them.

Natalie and Alan celebrated the birth of their son, George, in 1974. He was perfect in every way. Natalie enjoyed motherhood, fishing in the park with him, even trying to capture fireflies with him. She showered him with affection. But Alan did not approve of her 'nurturing' loving. He felt uncomfortable with her relationship with the baby.

"You need to stop all that baby talk when you play with my son. If he's ever to learn to be a man, he will need to be encouraged to be manly. If you make him a sissy, he'll never be much of a man!"

He saw the hurt look on her face, so he reiterated his comment. "Don't make him a sissy!" She knew he meant just what he said. He never tolerated her opinions or disobedience. She lowered her head as she lifted Georgie out of his crib. But now he was not Georgie ...just George. Alan saw to that.

She knew better than to go against his wishes. But *she* missed being held and cherished. She longed for the long passionate honeymoon kisses they shared on the Bermuda beaches. Now, the honeymoon was over and he had become all business. She appreciated the way he provided and cared deeply for his family. So maybe she did expect too much from him.

In 1984, Natalie unexpectedly was told by her doctor that she was pregnant again. George was nine years old and in the fifth grade. She was thrilled at the prospect of having a new infant to love. But Alan was not pleased. He reminded her that another child was *not* a part of his plans.

"How could this happen, Natalie? You *knew* we were only to have one child and now everything has changed." If only he would have welcomed the new baby. But he never gave her his love freely.

When Kathleen Pearson was born on October 10th, 1984, nothing could keep her from doting on her child. She didn't worry about making *her* a sissy! She was a dainty little girl and Natalie loved every bit of it... the dolls and the tea parties!

But Alan became more distant and his daughter hardly knew him. And George never accepted her.

When Katie had her 10th birthday party, George dreaded going to his parents' house for the celebration. The siblings were never close. It seemed to him his baby sister started her terrible two's and liked them so much she decided to stay there. She was spoiled and self centered. And George was a *very* mature seventeen year old. Her mother sacrificed to give her anything she wanted. So George resented having to buy her a gift, knowing she didn't need it and she probably wouldn't appreciate it.

Besides, his budget was too tight to be wasteful. But when the clock ticked around to 5:00 p.m., he drove to his parents' house... reluctantly.

That party was going to be the big event of the year for the 'little princess'... and the giggling little girls in Katie's class. George cringed thinking of coming face to face with a dozen little Katies. He had little tolerance for children, especially spoiled ones.

That night, the party started later than planned. The guests arrived and Katie was excited. The only one missing was her father. And he *never* arrived. That was the day that Alan Pearson decided to abandon his family and start a new life as though Natalie,

George and Katie had never existed.

Al Pearson was always known for his character, integrity and his honesty. He wasn't a rich man. He was seen as a prudent man, providing for his family well, but not wastefully. He took several pro bono cases.

George was proud to be his son; that is, until October 10th, 1994, on Katie's tenth birthday. Why did he choose to leave on Katie's birthday, in essence, just pushing her away? Katie's didn't understand, either.

Al and Natalie Pearson had been married for twenty-nine years and were never openly affectionate. But no one would have suspected that Al would leave his family and start over with Tina, the young law clerk in his office.

The woman was attractive but she had a whiney voice and seemed almost childlike in her admiration for her employer. It seemed unbelievable to think that a man as respected as Al Pearson would abandon his family, and leave them with nothing but his new fore-warding address in Henderson, Nevada, where he intended to start over with his soon-to-be bride.

Part 2 *George Pearson's Story*

George would never forgive him for abandoning his family! Then, he felt a wave of guilt engulf him, as though a voice whispered in his ear, reminding him of the times when *he* pushed his sister and even his mother away.

For the first time, he recognized that his actions were another form of abandonment, not allowing the family to form the connection that binds the heart of the family with love and trust. Now was the time to salvage the remains of their broken lives and try to start over. George was having a problem coping with that fact.

There were too many unstable factors and the anxiety was almost unbearable. He knew he needed to step up as the man of the house, to help recreate some stability to ease the burden on his mother, but for once his confidence let him down. He definitely wasn't ready to step into his father's shoes! He was a young man, albeit an *independent* young man.

On the night he graduated, his father presented him with his college fund. There was enough to pay his tuition and to purchase his books. With his part time job at the sheriff's office he was able to rent his own private home, which may be considered a luxury to some young college kids, but for George it was a necessity.

Natalie and Katie appeared to have created their own family since Katie was born, and George accepted the fact at a young age.

He was independent and adapted his life to suit his needs, as his father had done before him. He needed more time to revise his plans. But there *was* no time; His mother and Katie had to move out of the family's home and his mother had to return to work.

Stress and worry changed Natalie Pearson. Her heart was broken and she became fragile. For Natalie, her life had become fragmented; not at all orderly and protected like the comfort zone she had known. Her eyes stayed swollen as if tears had become a nightly ritual. But she never complained.

He wondered how much grief his mother could bear. George prayed to God to send angels to watch over her and for the Holy Spirit to bring her comfort, but he knew his faith was weak; he was bitter and angry with his father.

Pastor Hayden had warned him that weakness would come when forgiveness was withheld. "Being angry with someone, becomes self destructive, no matter why the anger is present. It's like a poison that consumes you, moving the grace of God further out of your reach. Soon all you can depend on is more pain and more resentment. You *must* be willing to forgive your father so God can get your lives back on track. He wants to put miracles in all your lives."

But all George could say to the preacher was, "I can't, Pastor. I'm just not ready for that yet." His life was full of worries and unanswered prayers.

Part 3 *Natalie & Katie Pearson's Story*

Katie was talking on the phone with her friends when suddenly there was nothing but silence. "Hello? Hello? Mom, this stupid phone is acting up again! Why can't we get a new one?"

Natalie was doing the breakfast dishes. As she picked up a dish towel, she turned to Katie slowly. "Sweetheart, it's not the telephone. I'm sorry, but our service has been disconnected. I knew it was going to happen but I just didn't know when."

Katie's eyes widened, "Mom, no! No phone? I *need* a phone! What will I tell everyone? Mom, how can I face all my friends?" Natalie searched for the right words, but the truth was the best she had to offer. I'm sorry, Katie! I didn't have the money to pay the bill." Katie slammed the receiver and ran to her bedroom.

Natalie heard her slam the door to vent her frustration. 'She will *really* be mad when the lights go out,' she thought. Last week Taylor County Utilities sent a final notice. Any day now, they would have no power and Natalie was trying to find a way to keep George from finding out. She vowed to never be a burden to her son. After all, he had his own life and it wasn't right to make him responsible for his mother and sister's hardship.

Natalie had been fasting and praying, expecting a miracle from God. She hoped to get it just any day now. She lowered her head with a little guilt as she admitted to herself that most of the fasting she had done was to save groceries for her child.

The doorbell rang and Natalie made a mental note to polish the old brass door knocker out front since the doorbell would be silenced when the electricity was gone. Katie yelled from her room, "If that's for me, I'm not here! I'm not leaving my room ever again!" Natalie smiled as she answered the door. Katie could be a real drama queen when she wanted to be. How she loved that daughter of hers! She gave her a reason to get up in the morning!

A man with a slight limp was leaving just as she opened the door, "Good morning! Can I help you, sir?" The man returned to the open door. "Ma'am, I am looking for Mrs. Natalie Pearson," he said as he looked down at the envelope in his hand. He looked up and smiled. She said, "I'm Natalie. And you are?"

She had a lovely smile, but very sad eyes. He laughed. Rarely did anyone care to ask for his name. "My name is Daryl, but I'm here just to deliver this letter to you. You have a nice day now." He shook his head, enjoying the brief encounter. He could see the pain in her eyes but she concealed it well. She was obviously a woman *'more valuable than rubies,'* as his employer would say, quoting Proverbs. His employer loved the scriptures!

Natalie looked down at the envelope addressed to her. This was a strange letter! The texture felt like a linen fiber. It had the feel of currency. In the upper left-hand corner was a pair of golden wings which held the three silver letters, NAJ!

As she slowly opened the envelope, she saw the legal documents. 'Dear Lord, please don't let this be divorce papers from Al.' He was in Nevada with Tina, but she refused his request for a divorce; she hoped he would decide to come to his senses and return to his family someday.

She wiped away a tear before Katie could see her crying. The documents were complicated, but it seemed to be a deed to property! Natalie shook her head, knowing it was too much to deal with now.

'Should I talk to George? No, he gets so mad at his father every time I go to him with a problem! It's not his fault. He's just angry for his father leaving us to manage alone.'

She thought for a second and then said aloud,

"Pastor Hayden! He'll know just what to do!" Katie came bounding down the stairs. "He'll know what?" Natalie shoved the letter into her apron pocket. Katie had forgotten she said she was never going to leave her room, and kissed her mother's cheek. I'm going to school, but I might go to Lorie's house *after* school, so don't fix my snack today, okay?"

Natalie always prepared some treat for Katie when she came home from school. Sometimes it was cookies or cake but lately a peanut butter and jelly sandwich had to suffice. Her food pantry was getting scarce so Natalie couldn't afford to bake as much lately.

She smiled as she realized that Katie left without even waiting for an answer to her question. 'Oh, well, just as well,' Natalie thought. She loved that about her. Nothing bothered Katie for very long. She just moved on to the next experience.... or teenage 'crisis.'

Pastor Hugh glanced at the envelope and saw it was like the one Bethany received. And the Jeffersons all reaped the benefits when Dr. Paul Santos was sent such a letter!

He held the closed envelope and asked, "May I open it?" She nodded quickly and anxiously watched him as he read the contents. She could tell that he was surprised more than once but he never made a comment.

He refolded the letter and reinserted it into the envelope. "Natalie, you are now the new owner of Liberty Square, the building Al first leased when he opened up his practice."

Natalie was shocked, "Why? What am I supposed to do with his office building? I can't even afford to stay in *this* house!"

Hugh smiled and shook his head. "No, Natalie, Al just leased the first floor. There are three floors. And the top floor is a six room apartment, with it's own private elevator, a sky light and patio garden!

The last time I saw the place, I noticed it was completely furnished with Oriental rugs and Italian leather sofas. It's like a mini palace!" Natalie was in shock! She began to pace nervously. "Who would give me such a gift? And why? Should I accept? Do I have any options?" She was still uncomfortable making any decisions since Al was gone.

Her mind was spinning with questions. "Natalie, I have seen the work of this benefactor before. He wants nothing in return but to remain anonymous. It simply means that you and Katie will be able to move into a new home with all the amenities!"

She sat down and stared at the pastor. "Is this even possible? Do I have to pay fees? I don't have any money, Hugh. Even my phone has been cut off. How can I do this?"

Pastor Hayden recognized that scared look on Natalie's face... he saw it in the eyes of the deer he hit with his pickup truck last November. She darted out in front of him and there was no time to stop. The grill on his pickup was damaged but he really hated seeing the fear in that helpless creature's eyes.

Hugh reached for Natalie's hand. Al left her so helpless! "It's going to be fine, sister. Give me the letter and I'll check it all out at the courthouse for you. You just start packing your valuables and we'll get you moved in."

Natalie said, "What about the utilities... electric, telephone, gas? I owe them a lot! I can't ask them to start new service and owe them like I do!" The pastor said, "If necessary, the church will help you pay for these expenses. But if I'm right, and I believe I am, this second document has given you an answer to all your financial woes."

Natalie started to cry but she smiled through her tears and said, "God still answers prayer, doesn't He, Pastor?" Hugh laughed and said, "He sure does!" The minister confirmed that all the documents were authentic and Natalie Pearson was granted the deed to the Liberty Square real estate. An account was set up to manage the building, it's maintenance and any restoration required, ten years ago, but the name of the account holder had been sealed by the courts.

All she needed to know as the new owner, was the ground floor was leased and brought in an income immediately to be transferred to her. And two of the offices on the second floor, were also rented out to be bringing in another check to provide for Natalie and Katie. The upstairs, which Katie would refer to as her new 'Penthouse,' would be their new home.

Natalie told Katie they were moving but she did *not* receive the news well. "What about all my friends? I'm not moving! I don't want to change schools! NO! *Mother, I am not moving!!* How can you be so mean?"

But she conceded to go and see where her *'mean mother'* would be living ... *'without her'*.. and she fell in love with *their* new home. Natalie's prayers were now answered! She thanked God for NAJ. But now Hugh Hayden was more determined than ever to find out who this NAJ was and why he chose the good people of Forest Hills for his project.

Part 4 *The Story of Katie's Friends*

Katie's friends were not impressed with her new address. She no longer qualified to be part of the elite teens from the exclusive estates. Katie was an outcast, rejected by all her 'friends.' But she was soon joined by a new group of 'non-elite' friends.

Jolee was the daughter of a seamstress and Micah's mother was a secretary. The only new friend who worried Natalie was Luke Avery. He was much older than Katie and no longer attended high school with her other friends. He lived at home with his widowed mother.

Natalie asked him once if he was a student at Katie's school. He smiled and said, "Not really. I used to go there but I guess you could say I enrolled in an institution for higher education." Natalie tried to force a smile and said, "Oh, like a community college ... I guess ... huh?" Luke just laughed and said, "Well, not exactly."

Katie slapped playfully at him saying, "Oh, quit

badgering him, Mother! Luke is okay the way he is, so just leave it alone!" Natalie agreed reluctantly.

"Ok, Dear, maybe I can just go fix us all some hot chocolate, all right?" Luke said, "Yeah, why don't you just do that ... *Mama!* Go whip up some *hot* chocolate for all of us!" Natalie felt her heart constrict as Luke grabbed Katie forcibly, laughing as he pulled her into his arms. He whispered something to her that made her blush. She laughed nervously and said, "You behave yourself!"

He released her and shrugged his shoulders, murmuring, "Hey, Baby, if you're hot, you're hot! And I say you got the kind of sizzle this man wants!" His leering comments made Natalie freeze in fear. She held her breath, and waited for Katie's response.

What attracted her to this older man? Why was she so fearful of Katie's friend? Was there even more darkness in his spirit than he let her see at this first encounter?

Katie, seeing the fear in her mother's eyes, said, "Mom, stop being such a prude! Luke is just fooling around! Tell her, Luke!" But he just stared with an icy glare in his eyes, and flicked his lit cigarette in her direction, sending it far across the room.

Natalie spoke to break the threatening silence. "Sir, I'll thank you to leave your cigarettes at home *if* you are invited back. I do not approve of smoking. We have a Christian home here."

The way he moved, the scowl on his face, all spoke volumes of disrespect and anger! She pulled her sweater closed, crossing her arms, waiting for him to react to her remark, but he just stopped and stared. Then, instead of showing anger, he laughed at her.

She blushed, wishing he would have been angry. She hated the way he tried to intimidate her. She wasn't sure where this relationship was headed. But the very thought of Katie being friends with Luke terrified her.

Natalie hurriedly excused herself and went into the kitchen to escape his hideous laugh. She decided she had to speak to George about Luke. In his line of work at the police station, he would surely know how to talk to someone like Luke. She heard Katie's voice.

"Mom, forget the hot chocolate, ok? I'm going to the mall now." Natalie was not willing to let her leave with Luke Avery. "No, Katie, you can't go out tonight."

She searched for a way to change the subject. "Look! You got a letter from the university today. At least open it before you go out." Katie turned to face her mother. She wasn't accustomed to anyone telling her what to do and she was outraged!

She grabbed the letter from Natalie's hand and glared at her, saying, "Luke just left, thanks to you, Mom! He said to tell you he doesn't need your attitude! I hope you're satisfied now, Mother! The 'Bad boy Luke' is gone!" Katie was furious with her.

Natalie was glad he left. She didn't want her to open it while Luke was there, anyways. She wanted to have a private moment with Katie to hear the news.

This was just one of several times when she missed Al. He knew just what to say and do to make all things calm and peaceful for her. He sheltered her from all harm, until *he* decided to shatter her life.

Her heart ached for the days when her family was all together. Her memory took her back to times when her children were little, reading Bible stories to them. She sang, "Father Abraham had many sons; many sons had Father Abraham."

Then she sighed as she blurted out that "Father Abraham's d*aughter* is tired of all this singing!" The comment brought rolling bursts of laughter from the whole family at the dinner table. How wonderful it was to share a laugh with the family!

She felt blessed at the dinner table. Al always said the blessing for them. Natalie looked at the bountiful feast spread out before them often, and she said another silent blessing, thanking God not only for the food but the family with whom He blessed her.

-45-

Moments of thanks were easy prayer starters, but spending quality time with God did not come easily for Natalie. Now, all her prayers started with just one simple word, "Please!"

Katie tore open the envelope hastily, then as she read the contents, her eyes grew wide with excitement, "YES! I got it! I'm going to school on a full scholarship! Mom, it's four years and all expenses! I can't believe it!"

She ran to call Jolee and Natalie was smiling, "I thank you, God for paid telephone bills!" She was happy Katie received such exciting news! Natalie put her hand on her heart, "Thank You, Lord!"

Katie ran for the front door, turned and said to her mother, "I know you said I can't go out tonight." She looked coldly at Natalie. "But I am old enough to make my own decisions now and I am *going* to the mall! I *may* return, and I may *not*! But either way, it will be *my* decision... not yours!"

Natalie was stunned. "Katie, I didn't mean to... I mean, listen, you just got some great news! Let's call George and we can celebrate, ok?" Katie sighed, grabbing her jacket as she slammed the door.

Natalie glanced at the clock; it would be dark soon and she worried about her safety. Four hours later, she was still gone. Natalie fell asleep on the sofa waiting up for Katie. At 6 a.m., Natalie was scared. 'She must have really been angry. She never came home last night.'

Natalie needed Al, but she knew he was gone so she decided to go to George's office to speak to him. She *really* needed his advice!

Part 5 *The Intrusion Story*

George planned every minute of his day so there would be no time for his mind to drift back to what might have been if his father had stayed. One thing was certain, George wouldn't be tossing and turning every night wondering if his mother and Katie were being adequately cared for. 'Just keep looking ahead and the past will take care of itself,' he reminded himself each morning.

And it usually worked, but not today, when his doorbell rang, interrupting his usual morning 'pep talk.' He glance at his watch. "Oh, no! I have exactly three minutes to be in my car or my day's schedule is thrown out of kilter!"

He picked up his jacket and coffee thermos from the breakfast bar with his left hand, his worn leather briefcase, a graduation gift from his mother (and from Katie), with his right hand and pulled the door shut behind him. Then he paused, and listened, satisfied the door had locked completely, before hurrying to his car.

"Excuse me, sir!" George was disturbed that his morning routine was changed. Everybody knew George needed consistency; change was not easy for him. "Sir, if I could just have a moment of your time..."

George was already backing his gray sedan out of the driveway onto the street. He stopped the car, annoyed with the intruder, and said, "I have no time now, sir! You will have to call my office later if it's really important!"

The businessman felt no umbrage. He just simply reached into his jacket pocket and handed him one of his business cards. "I won't keep you, but please call me at your convenience. I am an attorney. My name is Michael Genucci."

George hastily accepted the card as he called out, "Just leave a message on my phone, I really *must* be going, Mr. ....!" George hadn't forgotten the man's name; his memory was impeccable. He just refused to become familiar with anyone without careful scrutiny.

The young attorney said, "My name is Michael... Michael Genucci." George nodded abruptly, driving away as he placed the card in his vest pocket. But strangers were never welcomed inside his systematic life.

George knew there would probably never be a love in his life, for that would require him to open his heart to a stranger and allowing her in his domain.

And as far as 'What's- His- Name,' any man who had the audacity to invade someone's privacy deserved to be turned away. 'He said he wanted me to help?' But George shook his head in disbelief, 'I have a hard time helping myself. So you're on your own!'

But a Still Small Voice said to him, 'Is that what you learned from My word, Son?' George remembered Sunday school, 'More of Thee, Less of me, Let it be!"

Later, he would pencil in Mr. Genucci on his agenda. Now George was determined to get back on his schedule. He had fifteen minutes to get to his class.

Part 6   *Family Crisis Story*

Promptness was not the only thing important to George. He was determined to be an honest man, trustworthy... of good character. Al Pearson lost the respect and faith his son had in him when he left his wife and daughter. His character and reputation were destroyed. But George could not even admit to himself that he was crushed when his father left ... *him* !

He may be twenty-seven, but his heart ached as he remembered his father's voice and strong hands. He woke up often, dreaming he heard Al's commanding voice, forceful but full of pride for his 'boy.' In the morning he washed away the moisture; not *tears*, for George would never succumb to weakness.

Another day in the classroom, more tests, more assignments; George didn't mind familiarity that others deemed as monotonous or boring. At least he made it through one more day... successfully performing his job. George snapped his briefcase closed, preparing to leave the classroom.

He started to count off the 'to do' list as he did at the end of each day: '1. Thermos was washed and dried. 2. Test papers are neatly tucked in my portfolio. 3. Portfolio is in the first *top* section of my briefcase. 4. Day planner is in the second top section of my case. 5. Research data is in the side of my case. 6. File keys are in the side *storage* pocket in my briefcase. 7. House and car keys are in my *vest* pocket with... the business card left by Mr. Genucci. It's all seven checks now; seven, the Lord's number.'

George placed his hat on his head, and tapped it once lightly, without even realizing that Al Pearson made the same gesture each day. He left the classroom and as he pulled the door shut on his outer office he heard a familiar voice call out to him... 'George?'

He turned to see his mother walking towards him. When had she gotten so fragile? She was fifty-one but she looked much older. Her eyes were puffy; her step was slow.

"Can we talk, son? It's about Katie," she began to sob, "she never came home last night. I'm afraid she might *never* come home again!" George reached for his mother before she nearly collapsed in the hallway. He helped her into a chair and gave her some water.

"Mom, are you feeling any better now?" Natalie nodded and George asked, "Tell me, Mom, what's going on? Start over at the beginning." Natalie noticed her son's hat and apologized, "You were leaving, son, I'm sorry." She started to stand but George stopped her. "Mom, go on, tell me about Katie."

Natalie took a long breath and sighed, "I know Katie turned seventeen in October and she resented me for treating her 'as a child.' Even at seventeen, George, she *is* still a child! *My* child! Just like you are, George. Children never leave that place in their parents' hearts, even when they leave home."

George took his mother's hand, waiting for her to continue. "I wanted Katie home tonight with me. I was going to call you and see if you might bring a small cake and maybe some balloons so we could celebrate together.

Oh, I'm sorry, George, I'm getting ahead of myself! I meant to call you earlier today. Katie received her acceptance letter today! She was granted a full scholarship to the school she wanted to attend. She wanted to go into nursing, George. She was so proud!"

George sat back in his chair in disbelief, "Katie wanted to be a *nurse?* I never knew!" Natalie laughed, "She would have stopped you right there, George. She would tell you real fast that she was *not* going to be *A* nurse. Nosiree! She would be the *best* nurse ever."

George took his hat off and scratched his head in sheer disbelief. "Imagine that! Miss Katie Pearson, RN. I never would have guessed!"

Natalie told him how Katie left angry, believing she was old enough to make her own decisions. "I'm afraid I embarrassed her last night when one of her friends came to call. I know I wanted her to make new friends, but there's this one..."

She stopped, remembering that Katie went to the mall... as she had done so often! But then where did she go? "Well, Katie told me she may not come back home. I'm afraid she meant it."

George tried to reassure her, "Katie's just a kid, Mom. You know she's always changing her mind! She probably already forgot about last night and you are worrying about nothing." He saw by her reaction he hadn't convinced her.

"Look, Mom, you go home. Make a few phone calls to her friends and see if any of them may have seen her, okay? Then call me later tonight. It'll be all right." Natalie took a deep breath, "Of course, you're right.

But I was so scared when that man came to see her last night! She said they were just friends, but George, he's nearly *your* age! And he *smokes*! I just don't like him at all! I'm glad he left before Katie and I quarreled. George, we never quarreled before! But I *think* she went with her friend Jolee last night."

George waited she finished. "Mom, what *man* came to see Katie last night? And how is it that he's *Katie's* friend?" Natalie paused and searched George's worried face, "What is it, George? You think she could be in trouble, don't you? I think his name is Luke. I wish I could remember his last name. What on earth would a man his age want with a girl Katie's age?"

George was fully aware of the dangers a young woman could face today. His job with the sheriff's office brought him face to face with lots of men, both young and old, who would never give it even a second thought to rape or murder someone just on a whim. Katie should be grateful for a mother who cares as much as Natalie cared. Otherwise, she could be...

Suddenly, fear filled his heart. "Mom, what do you know about her visitor tonight? Do you know for *sure* if she left with someone? Where they live? A phone number? Try to remember, Mom! Do you have the names and the telephone numbers of any of her friends, someone she might have confided in..."

Natalie's eyes widened with fear. "Oh, no! You think something has happened to my Katie! George ... NO! Not Katie! She was alone last night when she left the house! She said she was going to the mall! Do you think she's in danger? Oh, George!"

George quickly shook his head, "No, Mom, wait! I don't know anything yet. But we need to get started checking on her whereabouts right away. I have some friends in the sheriff's office. Sheriff Randolph is the man I work with sometimes. Let me call him. Meanwhile, you put together anything you know that may help us find Katie."

He stood to his feet and hugged his mother, "So let's bring Nurse Katie home, shall we?" Natalie smiled and nodded as they walked through the melting snow in the parking lot. It was comforting to talk to George tonight. And this time he didn't bring up Al's absence and how he abandoned his family.

But her son was deep in thought as he planned his next move. He had Mitch Randolph's home phone number. He knew the sheriff would not mind his late night call. Then he would call Dean Winters' office and request a couple of personal days off. He was prepared to launch a full scale investigation, if necessary, until his sister was found safe and sound and returned to her home.

As they walked together, George placed his arm gently around his mother until they reached the blue Pontiac with the "Walking With Jesus" tag attached to the front bumper.

She believed the tag was a sign from God that everything would be all right. George remembered the day the bank repossessed her BMW after his father left. He also remembered the hateful names he called his father on that day.

But Natalie told George she didn't *really* need a car. She could take the bus or buy an older and less expensive car when she could afford it. The pastor's mother let her have the Pontiac when she bought a newer car for herself.

Not once did Natalie speak ill of her husband. And that was another reason George was so angry. But now was not the time to visit the past. He prayed with Natalie for Katie's safe return: "Dear, God, please build a hedge of protection around my sister until we get her back home safely. And Father, please teach me how to be the man I need to be to help my family be safe and protected.

Forgive my selfish, jealous heart. Give me this chance to be a good son and a protective brother for Katie. Help me become the kind of man who learns *what* my weaknesses are and *where* I can receive my strength, through Your Word and Your Mercy. Amen."

George hurried to his gray sedan, to begin his search for Katie. The night air was cold but his body ached from the tension he felt after receiving the news that Katie was missing.

That night he searched his rolodex for Mitch's number. Suddenly, the phone rang and it startled him for just a second. Lord, let her be at home where she belongs. He took a deep breath, preparing for the call.

"Hello, Mom, has she made it home? No? Well, do you have anything for me? Who she was with ... her friends? Anything?"

With fear in her voice, Natalie said, "George, I think she's with Luke... Luke Avery. She left with her friend, Jolee, after we quarreled. They went to the mall, but Jolee said she met up with Luke at a gas station later. That was the last time she saw her.

Oh, George, I'm worried! I found out Luke just got out of jail recently. We have to find her, George. I really don't trust him. I'm so scared!"

Part 7   *Search & Rescue*

The administrator at the college gave George a week off to deal with personal issues. Then he called a substitute to teach his classes and called to speak with Luke's probation officer.

He was ready to track every move Luke made since Katie disappeared. If they were together, he vowed to find them and bring Katie home where she belonged. She was long overdue for a talk from her big brother. And a few apologies, too.

The wind and rain was beating against his windshield as he drove cautiously through the Forest Hills section outside of town. The streets were not snow covered now but the freezing rain made the highway icy and he lost traction several times.

George had traveled the same route many times during his second year at the university, but today, he was having a hard time keeping his mind on the road. He saw a light from a roadside diner just ahead and turned on his left turn signal.

He worked with the warden at Forest Hills last year and he stopped at this same café every day on his way to work. He picked up a large cup of black coffee to fill his thermos every morning.

Edie Henson, the waitress, had his order and The Times Journal, ready for him at his table when he opened the door of the cafe. She always wore her red checkered apron and a big smile, knowing he would greet her with a cheery, "Good mornin', Good Lookin'! But today there was no cheery greeting.

George had a different reason for his destination today. He sat at the counter of the café waiting for his order, trying to compose himself. He had the over-whelming sense of dread that there may not be good news waiting for him at the sheriff's office.

Edie slowly approached him, knowing her friend was battling with problems hard to face. "Hey, Good Lookin'!" Edie called out but there was no response from her customer. "Are you okay, Friend?"

George tried smiling but she knew it was forced. "You look like you just lost your best friend! Will I do for a stand in?" Then, George's smile was real.

"Sorry, Edie. I'm just not myself today. My kid sister is giving my mom fits and I'm just hoping I can get her straightened out today." Edie shook her head, "Good luck, that's all I can say. That kid of mine! He has been causing me fits for years! Hey, if you come up with a magic antidote, let me know. I think I need a lifetime supply!"

George laughed and said, "Hey, maybe I'll just patent it and make a million!" Edie laughed and she pushed her pencil behind her ear. "Keep that smile, George, it fits your face real good!" He was still smiling long after he left the café. He really liked Edie. She had a way of lifting your spirits. 'That just goes to show you, everyone has their own set of problems,' he thought.

Maybe when all this was all over, he could offer to get Edie's son in the Big Brothers program. It sure worked wonders for some 'juvies' in the school system. He enjoyed working with the sheriff's office. If he had not already devoted so much to his teaching degree, he would have eagerly followed in Mitch's footsteps.

George's title was file clerk, but Mitch actually gave him his own cases to work. But today there was no caseload waiting in his cubicle. Not even messages from ex-cons. No meetings in the back room inside the warden's office, where he sometimes helped out.

Today, George would be searching for leads on the man who may or may not be responsible for Katie's disappearance. The sheriff at the station told him the files would be available to him, including the latest

-54-

updates on the missing persons files.

If there were any new clues, Sheriff Randolph would be the first to know. The deputies at the station took any tips from George quite seriously. If he sensed trouble brewing, they all kept an eye out for any hints of offenses.

He carried a caseload of nine clients. If he could work full time, he would have the quantities of files and workloads that brought complaints from the other probation officers. He listened to the others air their grievances and protests while envying their opportunity to make a difference in so many lives.

Mitch Randolph wished he had a dozen more like George. With his compassion and dedication it would make a big difference in his department, with repeat offenders like Luke Avery.

George enjoyed guiding some of the young men in his caseload to more productive choices. He helped some of the high school dropouts get their GEDs. At times his clients needed health care. Mitch respected his opinion and referred each case to the appropriate agencies.

George quickly made himself at home with the deputies. The men in the department considered him one of their own. They relied on his skills and the quirks that many misunderstood.

The job with the sheriff made him feel alive. As George ran into the station, the storm raged. The sleet pelted against his jacket and the sky was lit up with piercing bolts of lightning; thunder rolled and roared like a giant angry beast. The snow banks were mud and slush, beaten by the storm.

Sheriff Randolph stepped out of his office, when he saw him enter the station. "George, it's been a long time! Too long! I wish it were under better circumstances, though. Come into my office."

He poured his friend a cup of strong coffee. As George looked at the hot beverage he shook his head. "And I thought you'd given up on your destructive bad habits. This brew will kill ya!"

Mitch laughed, "Hey, they took away my smokes, my alcohol, and even started making me work out at the gym! They *ain't* getting my coffee! That's where I draw the line!"

George looked very serious, warning him, "My friend, that will never pass for coffee ... devil's brew, maybe." George made a face. "How long has that been bubbling in the pot?"

The sheriff laughed goodheartedly and said, "I sure missed having you around here. When are you going to give up that woman's work and come back here to do a man's job full time?!" George smiled.

How he missed these good times, just hanging out with Mitch and the men in the department! He gave himself a moment to remember how easily he fit in with the deputies but now George was ready for some action.

"It's times like this when I wish I did work here full time. I could use these files and check out all of Katie's dates before she got with the wrong kind!"

Mitch got a worried scowl as he said, "You mentioned Luke Avery. I ran a background on him after we spoke last night. I wish I had better news for you. That kid has been in trouble his whole life. He just got released the last time, about a month ago.

I can't see what the ladies see in him myself, but he's left his mark on quite a few ... black eyes, broken arms. If Katie's with him, she might have a problem ... a big problem."

George stood up quickly, tipping over his chair, "Let's go! Where does he live? Come on, Mitch! If he lays a finger on her I'll kill him!"

This was something Mitch understood and yet he also had to control the search. George's temper could cause Luke to go free. "No, I can't take you there, George. I know just how you feel, but you're going to have to trust me and the other men to bring him in to the station for questioning. It's gotta be handled by the book, my friend, or he could walk no matter what crime he's committed."

George impatiently paced the floor, "Well, what am I supposed to do while you're out looking for him? I can't just sit here by the phone!" Mitch stopped for a second.

"Well, *we're* going to check out the address we have on his record. Then *we* will question some of the hoods he hangs out with. Why don't you have a seat right there at my desk?"

George started to object but Mitch held up his hand, continuing, "You sit there and go through the case files on Luke. That way if we come back empty handed you may find something to get us back on track! Now doesn't that sound like a plan to you?"

It was beginning to make sense now. Everybody knew if there was a clue to be found, then George was the one who could find it. He reluctantly dropped into the sheriff's chair and tossed aside the files that were leading up to Avery's case.

"Luke Avery: Height: 5'10". Weight: 160. Hair: brown. Eyes: Hazel, Date of Birth: 07/04/1976. Nineteen seventy-six? Twenty-five years old? What on earth would he want with a young girl Katie's age?"

He sat back in the chair, closing his eyes. He had dealt with ex-cons like him before so George already knew why Luke was interested in Katie. He was just courting his next victim; and there was no way he was going to stay there while Mitch located Luke.

Glancing over at the computer printout on the sheriff's desk, he saw an address circled with a red pen: 1301 Elmwood Apartments on Amber Street. That was just outside Forest Hills. George was familiar with the area.

Wrecking crews were waiting for the orders to demolish the old apartments. He overheard Edie talking about it with one of her customers this morning. He wasn't really eavesdropping. She was bubbling over with her news she had qualified for a new home in Rose Court, built by some construction firm that sponsored low income families.

They gave her an option to buy the house as

rent. Edie was elated, especially since the apartment she shared with her son was going to be torn down. Now, she said, they would finally have a home of their own. It sounded a lot like the break his mother and Katie got on their blessing from NAJ, (whoever he is). They loved their new home. He thanked God for still looking out for His children. ('Hope found where hope was lost,' he heard that somewhere before, maybe in an old song.)

George smiled, remembering Edie bubbling over with excitement but his smile faded as he read more of Luke's information. Next of kin: Edith Sue Henson, mother. The emergency contact information listed the Forest Hills Café; ask for Edie. Unbelievable! Edie was Luke's mother?! This was the missing information the deputies needed.

George had the case file clutched tightly and the inmate data sheet in his hand, rushing to his car just as the sheriff arrived. One look at George told Mitch he found a clue the others had missed: "He's staying with his mother, Edie Henson, in the Forest Hills area! She's a waitress at the café outside of town. She has moved into a house on Rose Court."

Mitch turned on his heel to head back to his unit, but this time he had George hot on his trail. Nothing could keep him at the station now. He wanted to meet this Luke Avery, face to face.

George climbed into the passenger side in front while Mitch sped away from the station. Forest Hills was just about twenty miles away. While Mitch drove, George prayed. The sheriff waited until he saw him lift his head before asking questions.

"What tipped you off on Luke's address? His arrest record said he lived in those apartments. But no one there ever heard of Luke Avery or *any* Averys living there." Even the low lifes he hung out with were no help.

George told him, "Well, his mother just bought that house in Rose Court, so she's probably still moving her things out of the old apartment. Luke, too.

However, her name is Henson, not Avery. I have known Edie for some time but I never met her son, Luke. In fact, I just found out he was her son when I read his file. Mitch shook his head, "How did I miss that? That was a rookie error. I've been working in law enforcement too long to miss the name deal. I should have caught it."

George laughed and said in his best impression, "Stick with me, Big Guy! I'll show ya the ropes!" The sheriff gave him a sarcastic look, saying, "John Wayne, you ain't!" George smiled. "Maybe not, but Avery will think I am when I get my hands on him." Again, the older man shook his head, "You ain't doin nothin', George! You're just a passenger on this old joy ride! That boy is all mine... oh, *and* the law's!

Luke was standing by the mailbox when Mitch pulled up to the cafe where Edie worked. As the patrol car pulled to a stop, Luke made no attempt to run. "You lookin for me?" Mitch placed one hand on his revolver and said, "Should I be?" Luke shrugged, "I dunno. Seems to me when you guys got nothing better to do, you come lookin for me. I just thought I'd make it easy for ya this time."

The sheriff looked at his friend, "Ya know what I like about this job, George? Bringin' cocky punks like him down to his knees. Sooner or later, they all cry for their Mama. Ain't that right, little man?"

Edie came out of the cafe, as white as a sheet. "What's wrong, officer? Is my boy in trouble again?" Luke turned and pushed his mother away, "Go back inside, Mom, this ain't got nothin' to do with you."

Edie resisted Luke's force and turned towards George. "Tell me, sir. Are you here for my Luke? What has he done now?" George wiped the moisture from his eyes; not tears, because George would never succumb to weakness. "My sister, Katie is gone. Your son, Luke, was the last one with her."

Luke looked at him in disbelief. " You've got to be kidding! Are you crying?! You are wasting your time crying for her!? I did you a favor, man!" Edie stared at her son, shocked by his words, "Who *are* you!? I don't even know this monster inside you!"

Luke whirled around to his mother and lashed out at her. "When have you ever known anything about me? You're just like that whiny brat he's come for! You got to have a man to prove you're somebody! You never cared about me!"

Mitch reached out for Luke but he moved quickly, averting the sheriff's grasp. He laughed at them all. Deputy Frank Leacock, pulled up behind the sheriff's car but Mitch held up his hand, motioning for him to wait for his signal.

Luke wasn't done bragging. "Katie was a tease. She flirted and pranced around but when it came time to put out, she cried for Mama. Well, she ain't cryin' now."

George tried to grab Luke but Mitch held him back. It took all the strength he could muster but he had to keep George away from Luke. It was the only way to get a full confession from him. Let him believe that he was in control.

"Whadja do Avery? Drop her off somewhere? You didn't need her ... 'cause you can get lotsa women anytime ya want 'em, right? Luke laughed again. "You're right about that!" He shook his head, feeling smug.

"She thought she had me wrapped around her little finger but she looked down her nose at me like I wasn't good enough for her. Well, she was beggin' me to give her another chance! I hate beggars."

He turned to his mother who was trembling and pale, "Carl was *your* beggar, wasn't he, Mom? He'd do a*nything* to please you! He begged me to give him a chance. He said he wanted to be a father to me. All he wanted was to please you. I showed both of them!

Luke Avery is not here to be used by nobody! And that's just what they were! *Nobodys*! They both ended up crying and begging for my mercy! Well, I, Luke Avery, stood above their useless bodies until they had no more sniveling left. They got just what they deserved!"

Edie, sobbing uncontrollably, was helped into the cafe by friends. George was broken and sitting on the ground in tears. How could he have allowed his sister to be near this maniac? Mitch spoke in a slow controlled voice that came from years of dealing with hardened criminals, "I *can* believe you killed Carl but you haven't yet convinced me that you killed Katie Pearson."

Luke smiled and said, "Check the dump on Bailey Road. She's buried with the rest of the trash!" He turned aside as his neck gave a resounding crack; the next impact was Luke hitting the pavement. George had recovered enough to bring Luke down with one good upper cut.

Mitch looked at George. He slowly shook his head and said, "I hope you feel better, George, but if you hit him again, I'll have to report it, so *please* don't." He turned to Deputy Leacock and said, "I'll fill out all the necessary reports. You know nothing, got it?"

The deputy nodded, then pulled his hand cuffs as he read Luke his Miranda rights. "You have the right to remain silent. Anything you say or do can be held against you in a court of law. You have the right to speak to an attorney. If you cannot afford an attorney, one will be appointed for you. Do you understand these rights as they have been read to you?"

Luke never responded. Frank shrugged and added, "Oh, and Merry Christmas... Boy!" Mitch laughed, "I don't think he's conscious yet, Leacock! Just handcuff him, put him in the car and we'll read him his rights again on the way to the station.

Part 8   *The Pearsons' Sorrow*

Katie's body was found the next day. She had been brutally raped and her neck was broken. Luke was arrested for murder. George vowed to be a better son but he lost the chance to earn Katie's forgiveness.

The next few days were intense. The funeral was set for Saturday at 2 p.m. and George was overcome with grief. When guilt and shame didn't paralyze him, the needs of his mother filled him with exhaustion.

She was incapable of making any decisions without him. At times, he was able to talk her into lying down to rest, allowing *him* time to put the days ahead into focus, to gain a new perspective.

He tried to help occasionally, taking his mother out for dinner or picking up a few items at the market. But this brought shame to Natalie.

Being the wife of a prominent attorney, she never worried about finances, until her husband left her. And then, she had always been quite frugal, never asking her son for help. Now he was bringing *her* food and she was thankful but also humbled at the same time. Would she ever survive this pain?

How does a mother bury her child and then just walk away, and continue to live when her child has been murdered? And for that matter, how does a dad walk away from his own children and continue to live a life without any thought for their welfare?

She longed for her husband to return for years, still refusing to grant him the divorce he wanted. Natalie was sheltered and controlled her entire married life. Now, when he *wanted* her to make a decision, it was to decide if she would remain his wife. He would never get a divorce if it meant she had to agree to it.

Part 9 *A Father's Remorse*

Alan Pearson never cried so much in his life as he did when he heard of his daughter's death. All the remorse he felt consumed him body and soul. He had no one with whom he could share his guilt. He was a fool to leave his family to start his life over with Tina Moss in Nevada.

Tina wanted to marry him, but Natalie refused to sign the divorce papers setting him free to remarry. "You *know* there are ways to divorce your wife without her signing!" Tina badgered him constantly. "This is Nevada, for God's sake! Divorces and marriages are practically sold at drive-thru restaurants! What's really holding this thing up?"

Al wasn't sure why he couldn't proceed with the divorce. He just knew Natalie needed more time. Al tried to appease her with diamonds, flowers and even a new red sports car. But nothing he offered would satisfy her. Soon he realized that nothing would satisfy *him* in this relationship either. His whole reputation had been sacrificed for his lust and foolish pride; his family, home, and career were now burned bridges.

At first Tina hung on his every word because he was her idol. She bragged about his rugged looks, his stamina and his success. She constantly asked for his opinion on every subject she cared about.

Sometimes she amused him when she went on about an article she read on a celebrity. He said, "It's only gossip!" He wanted her to read more important material and to forget about all those trashy fan magzines she read. He suggested she might enjoy reading poetry; she told him he could read 'that book' to her sometime.

Everything spun out of control as their incompatibility grew daily. He watched as Tina sought comfort in the arms of another man. He could see his life replayed just by watching how she manipulated Jim's life, becoming a thorn in *his* marriage. He recognized her tactics... but a little too late.

Then one day, Al came home to a note on the refrigerator, 'Sorry to say goodbye but we just didn't work! Love, Tina.' He looked and all her clothes were gone, *and* her diamonds *and* the red sports car.

What a fool he had been! But you can't return by way of the bridges you have burned. You just try to make a life in the ashes that are left behind... and try to survive the haunted wasteland of your past life.

When he heard on the news about a young girl missing in Forest Hills, his heart broke for the family. He cried, knowing it *could have been* his daughter. When the reporter flashed her picture on the screen and gave her name as Kathleen Pearson, (Katie to her family and friends), he felt his heart stop. It *was his little girl!* He had to go home, burned bridges and all.

He had nothing left in Nevada, because he was never up to the task of reestablishing his reputation in the business. After he drained his bank accounts trying to buy Tina's love, all he had left were the memories... and the shame.

He knew he hit rock bottom when the landlord at the apartment they rented knocked on his door demanding the rent money. He gave Tina the money to pay the lease on their home for the rest of 2001. Now the landlord was losing his patience. The rent had not been paid since July and that was three months ago! Now Tina was gone with the rest of the money.

Al moved out of the apartment, and rented a shabby room adjacent to an all night diner. He shook his head, "If my friends could see me now!" He took a job at the diner to pay his rent and bought a used TV from a pawn shop with the last ten dollars from his paycheck.

He saw no way out of this nightmare he created for himself. He tried to pray but he stopped after saying, 'dear Lord.' He looked in the mirror and saw his shame in the reflection. 'Who am I... to think God would hear my prayers after the mess I made of my life?' He thought it was a miracle God didn't let him die for the way he destroyed the family he left behind.

When he heard his daughter was missing he screamed out to God from his agony, "God, NO!! It should have been me! Not Katie!! She's just a little girl. I haven't even told her I loved her! Oh, Lord God, what have I done? Merciful God, what have I done!"

Al laid on the floor of his rented room, next to the café and cried out to God. When he didn't show up for work, Buck, the grill cook, came to check on him. Seeing him on the floor, he shut the door again and wrote him off as another unreliable drifter. It was probably drugs or the bottle that brought him down.

But Al never resorted to either. He was lost in

a bad place, where no man should ever end up, but drugs and alcohol were not at fault. His daughter was gone and he should be there leading the search!

He checked his wallet. He saw six dollars, but no hope. He heard the knock at his door but there was no one he cared to see. Surely, they would leave if he ignored them. But a few minutes later, Buck came and unlocked the door again with his key.

"Hey, Buddy, whadja do, lay out all night? This man's been knockin' so hard, the walls of the diner shook! You better talk to him. It might be important, Bud."

(When Al asked for an application for work, old Buck said, I don't need no application, you got the job." Al said, "You don't even know who I am. Don't you want my name?" Buck laughed, "All you drifters are Bud as far as I'm concerned. That way I don't have to order a lot of new name tags when you move on." It made sense to Buck and Al didn't care.)

Now Buck was staring at him, waiting for him to talk to his visitor. The grisly cook sat down and he waved his hand signaling 'Bud' to speak. But Al stood up and said, " Thanks, Buck, for all your help, but I think I can handle things on my own now."

Buck slowly got up to leave, and glancing back at Al, said, "If you need me, I'll be at the grill." Al smiled and said, "I know. See ya later, Buck." He waited for the door to shut. The old cook was still standing outside trying to listen in, so Al walked to the door and waited, watching to make sure he went back inside the diner.

Satisfied that they were alone, he returned to his visitor. "I'm sorry about that. Buck just likes to know everybody's business. So now why are you here to see me?"

The man walked across the room and Al saw he had a slight limp. "I just need to make sure that you are Alan Pearson from Forest Hills. Do you have any identification?" Al eyed him suspiciously, "I might say the same to you, sir. Now, who are you? And why are you looking for me?"

The man smiled as he dropped his head. "I'm sorry, my name is Daryl and I'm not usually this mysterious. I guess it was the flight. I'm used to driving everywhere and this is a little different for me. Give me a second to get grounded, ok?"

Al relaxed and waited. Daryl pulled an unusual envelope from the inside pocket of his jacket. Al's curiosity was peaked. The envelope appeared to be made of some sort of linen fiber and there were gold angel wings in the upper left-hand corner. The wings seemed to be encircling three silver letters that shimmered... N...A...J.

"I will leave this delivery for you to read. It's self explanatory." He reached for Alan's hand and he shook it warmly. Smiling, he said, "Have a good day, sir." Before Alan could respond, Daryl was gone. And there were so many questions unanswered! He glanced down at the special delivery he received.

What an odd letter! Al slowly opened the letter and found a one way ticket home! How could this be? But there was another letter that had beautiful hand-written script, telling the story from Luke 15.

"The Father welcomed home his son who had squandered all his fortune on wild living. He came to his senses and in humility, he saw his foolishness. He repented and His Father received him again with open arms, full of compassion. Come home, Son, your Father is calling for you. His servant will help you as you complete your journey." Al broke down, sobbing, repenting of his sins.

Part 10 *The Homecoming Story*

The woman at the ticket counter at the airlines reached for his ticket, and smiled. Most of the travelers had come to Nevada to gamble at the casinos in Las Vegas or Reno. She had a greeting for each customer with a friendly smile and the usual question, "Are you going back home?"

Some of the passengers remarked they had to go home; they were too broke to go anywhere else! She smiled at Al Pearson and asked, "Going home?" "Yes," he replied, "Praise God, I'm going home." His eyes brimmed with tears.

Pastor Hugh was visiting the nursing home on the outskirts of town. He hadn't visited Ralph Curtis for a couple of weeks and the old war veteran was on his mind lately. Ralph was overjoyed to see him.

They visited and chatted about his bygone air force days in World War II. He loved to tell his old war stories. Hugh was a great listener, even though he heard all the stories several times. He prayed for Ralph and when he stood up to leave, he heard someone say, "The airport is down the road a mile or so."

Hugh responded with, "Yeah, I know, I used to go there as a boy with my dad and watch the planes come in for a landing." Ralph looked a bit confused. "Pastor, are you all right?" Puzzled by the question, Hugh said, "Yes, I'm fine. Why do you ask?"

The old man hesitated, then explained, "'Cause I said the Big War was the worst but Nam would be a nightmare. Then you said you used to go there as a boy with your dad to see the planes land."

Hugh gave a forced laugh and said, "I guess my mind wandered for a moment." He said, teasing, "I guess I'm getting old, Ralph!" The old man shook his head, laughing and walked his 'old' friend to the elevator. The pastor hugged his friend.

"Come back soon, okay, Hugh? I value your friendship." As the minister left, he wondered about the voice he heard! Where had it come from and why?

He started to turn right at the stop sign to go back to town but paused, remembering, 'the airport is just down the road a mile or so.' He changed his mind and as he steered his car into the left turning lane, he watched for signs directing his lane into the airport terminal. He searched for the designated areas for a place to park his car.

He locked the doors and started walking towards

the observation entrance. Suddenly, he heard his name called, "Pastor Hayden? Is that you? You're a sight for isore eyes!" The minister saw the man from a distance and for a minute he thought it looked like Al Pearson. Then he confirmed it.

Alan's eyes were deep sockets; his clothes were rumpled. He was thin and his shoulders seemed to be carrying the weight of the world on them. "Welcome home, brother!" Hugh knew this man had faced many demons but now he had come home at last! Alan had come home for his family!

"Hugh, did they find Katie? I saw on the news she was missing." The minister stopped and apologized, "I'm sorry, Al. I thought that was why you were here today. There's no easy way to tell you this. Katie was found, Al. But she was murdered. Her funeral is... this afternoon. I am so sorry for your loss!"

Al sat down his one suitcase and dropped to the curb. "My God, look what I've done to my family!" Hugh held him and let him cry. "Why don't you come to the parsonage and freshen up? You can come to the church with me later, if you like, or come when you're ready. Did you rent a car or call a cab?"

Hugh looked around when Al spoke. "No, I was told you would be here to pick me up. At least, I was told someone... did I miss something?" Al reached into his pocket for the treasured envelope, and Hugh knew why he was drawn to the airport. "No, of course not. Let's go if you're ready." Some day, Hugh would solve this mystery!

Al showed up for Katie's funeral alone so Pastor Hayden led him to Natalie and George at the front of the church where they sat for the service.

George was angry and would have insisted the pastor send him away, but he saw his mother's eyes, hollowed and full of tears. She needed him to be there and George would not deny her that small comfort.

"Thank you for having me," he said humbly. "I know I don't deserve any consideration and I'm not asking for your forgiveness. There is no excuse for all the hurt I've caused this family. But if I had all those years back to do over..."

George motioned to his father to stop. He knew his mother could not deal with any more problems, at this time of loss. And he was fighting back the urge to blame him for Katie's death. Had he been there, Luke Avery would never have stepped foot in their home!

No, George wasn't ready to listen to anything he had to say to them. As far as he was concerned, Al Pearson burned all his bridges and there would never be a time for crossing back over them!

Hugh Hayden stood by the casket, preparing to start the service. Death was the hardest fact of life to bear; but it is a part of God's plan for all of us. He looked at the family, full of anguish and he wondered how God would mend this broken family. But always the question in his mind would be '*how*' and not '*if*'.

As the church filled with mourners, the pastor opened with words that shocked even himself: "Good afternoon! This is the day the Lord has made. Let us rejoice and be glad in it..." Almost inaudibly, he said, "Psalm 118:24."

Did he just use *that* scripture? Today? At the funeral of a young girl who was brutally murdered? Was he crazy? Hugh Hayden looked around in the sanctuary and saw the odd reactions on the faces of the mourners staring at him. He prayed silently, 'Lord, get me out of this!'

"I realize that I may have just shocked some of you with the text I have chosen. But the Lord is now directing me through His Spirit to remind you that God *is* still in control. He is *still* the Creator."

Hugh took a breath and said, "We could learn from Katie's life. She loved everyone unconditionally." He thought to himself, 'and it was probably the same misguided trust that brought evil into her life which eventually led to her death.' He continued, "Katie had never held a grudge."

Hugh Hayden cleared his throat. "I remember when she shared an observation with me that I will never forget. I stopped her on the way to her Sunday school class one day. She was eleven or twelve years old. I knew she had problems and struggles in life, so I wanted to let her know she could come to me if she needed to talk.

I said, 'Katie, we may never know why God lets us go through trials in life but after the tears victory will come if we trust in Him.' She stopped for a mere second as though she was considering what I said. And then she replied, 'Pastor, these aren't *just* tears. God told me they were raindrops that He makes in heaven. When we get thirsty for His comfort, then teardrops are sent to get us through our sad times.' "

George remembered when Hugh explained why tears were needed to heal a broken spirit. He said. "A very wise person once told me that God sent tears as raindrops to water our valleys, to quench our thirst and to receive His strength... teardrops from heaven!" He was talking about Katie!

Hugh Hayden stopped to wipe his eyes and he smiled, saying, "Katie's raindrops," as he held up his handkerchief. He stopped as he looked to the pew where Al, Natalie, and George were seated.

"Katie knew how to love, because she knew to forgive. I'm not asking for forgiveness today for the man who took her life. It's far too soon for that. But grief is a consuming force and unforgiveness builds a prison wall around hearts allowing only grief to live inside. Bitterness stands guard and rejects peace."

He paused waiting for the next words to come to him from God. "So today this casket will be buried. Only Katie's empty vessel will be interred, (because she's not here, she's with the Lord). Katie is beginning her eternity, and it seems only appropriate that we all prepare ourselves for a new beginning. Let us search our hearts and make room for Jesus Christ, our Lord and Savior. Invite Him into your heart today."

The pastor paused, looking around the church. "And if there be any among us who has 'aught...' (or 'anything') against a brother... or anyone, we need to deal with it now.

Put all those hard feelings to rest and start anew. God cannot forgive us unless we can forgive others. Without forgiveness, there is no repentance; without repentance, there is no salvation. And without His salvation, there is no eternity in heaven with the Lord Jesus Christ. No hope, no rest for weariness...no... peace. Do this in honor of Katie... hold tight to love."

Hugh Hayden looked around the room and he noticed that many had received his message, including the Pearson family. He took a deep breath and slowly, reverently... said, "Let us pray."

The days following Katie's funeral were somber. George returned to his teaching. Natalie went back to Liberty Square to care for her tenants. Alan Pearson took a room in Miller's Bed and Breakfast on the outskirts of town.

Corene Dudley's parents had owned the inn but they couldn't keep up the maintenance. She told Al he was welcome to stay but the rooms were nothing like he was used to. And it might get a little noisy with all the remodeling! Al replied, "You might be surprised by what I've grown accustomed to. Your place will be perfect until I can get back on my feet again."

The season was changing and life was stirring in Forest Hills. Natalie received notice her ground floor tenant would be moving in two months. A new Commerce Center was under construction and the firm would be their first tenant. This, of course, meant she would be looking for a tenant to take over the lease.

The pastor was counseling the Pearsons since Al came back home. Al never realized how much Natalie had to offer their union but she never had any faith in her own judgment.

This time of separation had been hard for them. But each of them grew in wisdom, in strength of their character and self confidence.

Natalie agreed to lease her prime rental property to Alan Pearson, *the Attorney At Law*, (for a fair price). She even made sure he read all the fine print in her contract while sitting in her office!

And Hugh was sure the subject of a prenuptial agreement came up... by Natalie! Alan proposed to Natalie again. He wasn't asking her to renew their vows; he wanted a whole new beginning.

George still had a problem accepting his father back in his life, but he was willing to work at it. But he wouldn't have a lot of free time. He was taking the position as houseparent at the Sheriff's Boy's Ranch for adolescent males who were first time offenders.

Mitch felt a mentor like George would be just what they needed. When George reported for the interview, he carried a reference letter from the college. He had excellent credentials and his work with the sheriff made him an ideal candidate. At least, that's what Dorothy said.

She was the nurse who came to see the young men each month. She was attractive (and single). He wondered why she never married. She was extremely conscientious! Everything in her briefcase was labeled, color-coded and cross-referenced. She was perfect!

He asked how she found her job opening at the facility and she told him the strangest story about a linen envelope... with golden wings and silver letters that said, NAJ.

-

Chapter 5 ~ *Mitch's Story*

Sheriff Mitch Randolph, in uniform, stood behind George, service revolver at his side, as usual. He was a good friend to George, but it was hard for him to spend his life among hardened criminals, then become a civilian in a peaceful world. The civilian place was where his own little girl, Meagan lived, alone with a mother who was terrified of weapons and police calls. It was a safe place where one attended the ballet and operas and picnicked in the green valleys of Bonn, Germany.

Mitch was not a part of that place, and yet it held his most valuable possession, his heart. Would he ever hold his child again? And his wife, Lily ... if only he could hold her in his arms, one more time ...

Mitch wiped the tears from his eyes. It would not look good for an old cop like him to be caught crying. He reserved his tears for the nights, with the lights out.

He had a cabin on a lake. Lily teased him and said what sold him on the real estate was the name ... Lake Warden. She said he was obsessed with his job, which he knew could not be farther from the truth.

If Mitch had his way, there would never be a need for police officers. Everyone would look out for each other and all the prisons would be shut down. But he knew realistically, it would never happen! And every year, the crime rate increased. All the public could do, seemingly, was to gather up the corpses of loved ones, like Katie Pearson, and plan their funerals.

Lily tried to live in her husband's world. For five years she stayed and did her best to be a good cop's wife. But when she heard the sirens, she sensed her husband was facing danger. But even that wasn't the reason she decided return to Germany with Meagan.

Mitch trusted no one. He suspected everyone he met. He had files at work on all criminal activities and he knew all the dark secrets and family skeletons of nearly everyone in Forest Hills. He even knew when someone got a parking ticket. He was nearing paranoia and that was when the arguments started.

Lily was too trusting and Mitch was not willing to trust anyone. Every time Lily went shopping with Meagan, she had to listen to a briefing on being extra cautious. "Keep your doors locked at all times, Lily. And if anyone tries to get you to pull over, don't do it! You drive to the nearest emergency facility. Go to a safe place... a fire department, a hospital, or a police station and report the perp!"

If she came home late, he paced the floor waiting for her to get home and an argument always ensued. But Mitch usually left before the words escalated to a full blown battle.

Lily confronted him once when he returned after one of their fights. She heard his key in the lock in the early morning hours. She asked, "If you are so worried about us all the time, how can you leave us out here alone on the lake all night?" His answer was, "I didn't leave you alone. I sat in my car, all night watching you." She knew then, she had to leave him.

Lily had been homesick for years. Her father was stationed in Germany in the early 1960's, when he met Lily's mother, Greta. They had a storybook wedding. Her father dressed in his dress blues and Greta wore the wedding dress worn by Lily's grandmother. For three generations, Lily's family carried on the customs and handed down heirlooms to be treasured forever.

Lily's father retired from the U.S. Army and he chose to make his home in Germany. He blended easily with the German people and chose to raise his family in Bonn.

When Lily met her *own* soldier, it appeared that history was repeating itself. But Mitch left the marines after his first hitch and returned to the states. Lily was heartbroken.

"Mama, I love Mitch. I thought we would get married! How do I live without him? I miss him so very much." Lily was heartsick. "You and Papi are very happy, Mama. That is what I want to have with Mitch." She fell into her mother's arms, crying. Lily's mother had words of wisdom for her daughter. She told her to follow her heart.

Mitch wrote to Lily and told her how much he loved her and wanted her to be his wife. But his home was in America. She would have to leave her family and her beloved country to be with him.

So she said her tearful farewells at the airport and new tears of joy greeted her in America. Mitch and Lily were married right away, on the following Saturday afternoon at 3 pm, on June 27th, 1981. But there were no military wedding plans, and there were no celebrations with her lifelong friends.

She brought Oma's (grandmother's) wedding dress but decided against wearing it. Somehow she felt it would be an act of betrayal to wear the precious gown of her traditional German heritage to wed in a small church in America.

There were just forty guests in attendance and she only knew a few of them. Members of the church came to make her feel welcome. The secretaries and deputies attended from the office but it was not the wedding she dreamed about when she was a little girl.

Mitch took her to the cabin on Warden Lake for their honeymoon. It was almost as if his bride was an afterthought, an insignificant addition to his life. She wanted to be the *reason* he woke up each morning, and not someone who just moved into his house.

When the doctor told Lily she was pregnant at Thanksgiving, she couldn't wait to tell Mitch. She had dreamed of tea parties and ballet with her own little princess. Mitch was thrilled! He was so thrilled he installed security lights and an alarm system complete with cameras as a way to keep his precious little girl safe in his world. And again, Lily cried.

How could they be so different and yet love so

deeply? Mitch worshipped the ground Lily walked on and Lily was very proud of Mitch and his bravery. He was loyal to family, friends and country. There were no limits to his generosity and love. He had so much to offer, yet Lily was missing her family and her country.

When Meagan was born, on the 26th of August in 1987, she filled a big portion of the hole Lily felt in her heart; it just took a smile from that tiny face, the way she held to Mama's finger and how her big blue eyes searched for the sight of Lily. Her golden curls formed dainty ringlets that framed in her rosy baby cheeks. She giggled and cooed. For just one second, Lily was satisfied, content to be in America, married to Mitch.

At first, Lily was afraid she would never have children. Meagan was born after six years of trying to conceive; she promised God she would treasure the little life he gave to her.

When Meagan began walking, Mitch as afraid for her safety. What if a stranger tried to grab her? If she smiled that adorable dimpled smile of hers would some pervert try to kidnap her?

Mitch was determined to protect her around the clock. He would spare no cost or effort to keep his wife and baby safe. It became an obsession with him, and Lily could take no more. She took Meagan and returned to Germany in November, 1995. Meagan was eight years old.

Mitch's heart was broken and his friends began to worry it might destroy him. He began drinking and taking chances on the force; not anything that would jeopardize his deputies, just himself.

He stepped into the line of fire once and took a bullet in the chest. He said he was trying to distract the gunman who was robbing the local convenience store. Mitch nearly died. He was in surgery for over nine hours.

After recovery, the department insisted that the rehab therapy would not be enough. He had to follow

the doctor's strict orders: Exercise at the gym, no
alcohol, throw out the smokes and lose weight. It was
exactly what Mitch n*eeded* to do to get his life back.
It was just what Mitch *hated* to do to get back a life
that now excluded his wife and daughter.

Now, as Mitch walked away from the graveside,
he wondered if Lily ever talked to Meagan about him.
Did his wife and daughter know how he struggled to
get through the night, knowing they were gone? That
each morning his pillow was wet with the tears he
shed in the night? Did they know he didn't want to
live another day alone... without them?

Time was so precious! Meagan was eight when
Lily took her back to Germany. He hadn't seen his
daughter for six years. Meagan was a teenager now!
All those years were wasted as his little girl grew up
without her daddy who lived on another continent.

Mitch wiped away a tear and swallowed the lump
in his throat. 'Oh God, please... you surely have an
answer for me. I can't go on without peace.' Then the
lawman returned to his patrol car, on the job one
more time.

His wife and daughter were gone but he had
to go on with his life in Forest Hills. He turned onto
the highway with the intention of going back to the
office when a semi came around him with air horns
blaring.

He had foolishly pulled out into the line of traffic
without seeing the big rig. His first instinct was to pull
the driver over for exceeding the speed limit. But then
how could he explain why he pulled into his lane? He
also didn't want to tell anyone why he was crying. So
he let the incident slide, vowing he would pay closer
attention to the road!

Within a mile, he saw a vehicle pulled off the
road, with the hood raised and decided he needed to
stop. After all, he *was* a public servant. It was now
time to put his personal problems aside.

The driver was walking around the old 1985 Lincoln Town Car. He had a noticeable limp. His pass-

enger, who remained in the back seat of the car was an older male, probably caucasian.

Mitch approached the vehicle and parked his cruiser behind it. After placing a call to dispatch to run a check on the tag, he reported he was making a citizen contact. He was not going to take any more chances; he slowly approached the car, and looked for any indications of danger. He had been in law enforcement long enough to know it only took one mistake in judgment to become a casualty.

"Good afternoon, sir! Is there a problem?" The driver smiled at the sheriff. "Well, my passenger said I needed to pull off the road and raise the hood. But I don't hear anything or see anything wrong. I guess better safe than sorry, though."

Mitch rsponded, "Yes, sir." Then he asked him, "Could I see your driver's license and registration, please?" The man limped to open the passenger side door. Reaching inside the glove compartment, he retrieved the packet that contained all the documents pertaining to the vehicle. "Here's the registration card, a valid driver's license (for Daryl Baker), and the insurance card." He placed an envelope with them.

Mitch looked at the driver's documents, saying, "Thank you, Mr. Baker; everything appears to be in order." He handed the papers back to the driver but he hesitated when he saw the envelope included in the packet. Daryl knew it was addressed to the sheriff. Mitch returned everything to Daryl but held out the envelope in his hand, and asked him, "What is this?" Daryl shrugged, "It doesn't belong to me. Am I free to go, Officer?"

Mitch nodded and he waived him out onto the highway, still a bit puzzled by the envelope, with the texture of paper money. There were golden wings in the upper left-hand corner that encircled three silver letters, NAJ.

Lily was lonely and yet she refused to divorce Mitch. She told him she and Meagan would wait for when he chose to be a part of their lives. He wrote to them weekly in Germany but it was not nearly as good as having him there with them.

Sometimes Lily wondered if she made the right choice in leaving, but all she had to do was look for the sparkle in Meagan's eyes to see that no sacrifice was too much. She was the light of her life and the beat of her heart. She knew Mitch would have made them prisoners in their own home. He smothered them with his fear for their safety. No, this was the only way.

If only he would have visited them in Germany to keep his memory alive in Meagan's heart. She even stopped asking the questions that broke Lily's heart: "When's Daddy coming home?" and "Why can't I see my daddy?"

She became adjusted to her new life and her father was her past. Lily knew by his letters that he wanted to come for a visit. But there were many reasons why it just wasn't possible.

He had accumulated plenty of leave time. He saw no reason to take time off. He had to stay busy or he'd find himself drowning in a 'What ifs and I wish I had...' pit.

So how could he give Meagan any false hope? He knew it would break her heart (and his) when he had to say goodbye again. Plus, he held Lily in his arms every night now when he closed his eyes. She left the scent of her body on his pillow each morning. He knew it was just a dream but still it was really a beautiful dream, more comforting than some of the scenarios he envisioned in real life.

Would reality be any better for bringing comfort to his world? The fear of losing what little he had now was a horrible thought! Would she try to send him away? Would she tell him she couldn't live alone anymore? Would she want to marry someone else, maybe someone who could hold her close when the storms were coming? He knew how crashing thunder frightened her.

Then, he could not forget the harsh reality of

international airfare. Last week he paid a roofing company to replace some shingles on his cabin, and had to look twice at the bill. He half jokingly said, "You are just *repairing* the old *roof*, right? I'm not planning on building a new house in the near future." He looked again at the bill, $4,000! He knew he had to have the repairs but it took a big bite out of his bank account.

If he had to pay for the trip to Germany, he would have to be very careful with his budget there. No, he couldn't go see his daughter for the first time in six years as a pauper. He wasn't a spendthrift but he would at least like to be able to take her to the ballet. She *loved* the ballet! And dinner at a nice restaurant!

Oh, who was he kidding? He never would have a chance to go to Europe on his income. He should have *never* said goodbye to his family! It would be hard to make up for six years of separation.

Mitch pulled into his driveway, got out, and as he locked the car door, he saw the letter still lying on the seat. It was probably some firm eager to make a good impression with their ad propaganda. But as he retrieved the letter, he realized, the envelope was too expensive for junk mail correspondence. What a logo in the left hand corner of the envelope! Gold wings? Silver letters?

Carefully he opened the letter. The envelope felt like currency! As he carefully unfolded the letter, a card fell to the ground. No, it wasn't a card! It was a ticket! He picked it up and read the flight number and the departure date scheduled for December 22nd!

This flight would take him to the Cologne/Bonn Airport and he would go by train to his destination! Lily's arms! For Christmas! The railpass was included in a file inside the envelope. The letter instructed him to check in with Rachel Madison at the Visa/Passport office located in Richmond, Virginia, within five days. Was this a con?

Mitch called the airport in Richmond. He was on

the passenger list! Then he called the Passport office. "I would like to speak to Ms. Rachel Madison, please. Mitch Randolph calling from Forest Hills." While he waited, he wondered who was behind this. Whoever it was, he was very thorough in setting up his mark!

"Hello, Rachel Madison here. May I help you?" Suddenly, Mitch was at a loss for words. "Well, my name is Mitch Randolph and I was instructed to request to speak to you at the Visa/Passport office. I'm really not sure who has made these arrangements for me. Can you fill me in?"

He didn't want Lily to pay for his trip. He was never comfortable asking anyone for help! "Did you say the name was Mitch Randolph? Let's see, I have a tentative time frame established. I won't be in the office after the 20th, so I'm trying to see all my clients before that date. Would you like to schedule a firm appointment now?"

Mitch shook his head to clear his thoughts, and said "Ma'am, I don't know what the *appointment* is actually about. Who is paying for this? Can you enlighten me at all?" She sounded confused, "Uh, Mr. Randolph, did you receive the airline ticket and the railpass? You should have received them this afternoon."

He answered, "Yes, Ma'am, I did but I..." She interrupted him. "Sir, you *must* have a passport if you intend to travel to Europe." Mitch started to speak, "I know, but who..."

She said, "Will you be making your appointment with me now, sir?" He was speechless. "Sir, so far I have this Monday morning at 11:00 a.m. available, if that suits you. And don't forget, you will need two forms of picture IDs. Mitch stammered, "Of course, but... I..."

Is there anything else I can do for you today?" He simply said, "No, Ma'am, I guess that's all I'll... need today." She replied, "I am looking forward to meeting you. Have a wonderful weekend, sir." And the line was silent.

Mitch went over the events of the day in his mind. 'What is going on here? How? Why? Is this even possible?' He called the dispatcher and heard him laughing. So that was it! They were just playing a joke on him at the station! "Ok, so you had me going! But your paybacks are coming!"

The dispatcher tried to stop laughing, "Yeah, right, Mitch! And I guess next month you will be going to Hawaii for a 'period of time.' That has got to be the oddest request for leave time I have ever seen! You really hired a company...NAJ... to send us a *telegram*, no less, informing us that you will not be in the office for an 'undetermined period of time'? We're still laughing!"

Mitch was not amused. "Oh, yeah? Ya wanna hear something really funny? This will have you rollin' in the aisles! *I didn't send it!!*" Then he slammed the receiver down!

He was still frantically pacing the floor in frustration when George Pearson came to his door. He tried to explain the mysterious letter to him and said, "What is happening here, George? Am I going nuts? Have you ever seen anything so crazy?"

George Pearson needed this distraction. "Yes, as a matter of fact I have." Mitch looked at his friend and said, "Is it for real?" George nodded, "My pastor, Hugh Hayden, helped my mother when she received *her* letter. He confirmed it's all legit.

Someone just senses somebody's need and then answers it! That's about all I can tell you! If you call Pastor Hayden, he'll tell you what he knows about it. So when are you leaving?"

Mitch hung up the phone. His friend, George was right. But he had to give that minister credit! Even if all the details checked out and the gift was authentic, (albeit mysterious), he would not be satisfied until he got to the bottom of it.

Who was NAJ? And why was he so generous with Hugh's people? Or did it extend beyond Forest Hills? And who is financing all this? Mitch told the man of God, "When do you find out, sir, let me know. We will either hug his neck or wring it!"

Hugh Hayden smiled. He always liked the sheriff and he couldn't think of a more deserving recipient of the benefactor's gift. Mitch needed his family and this was possibly the only way to reunite them. He thanked God for answered prayer.

Mitch met Rachel Madison and she confirmed that his passport was in order. She even managed to get a Visa stamp for his stay in Germany. She said NAJ ordered the stamp as a part of the package.

Mitch saw his chance. "Great! And who is NAJ?" Rachel paused and asked him, "You did bring the envelope with you, didn't you? I'm sure you had a letter of introduction inside."

"A letter? Inside the envelope? I didn't see any letter." He pulled the strange envelope from his suit pocket and Rachel took it from him. As she reached inside the envelope, she removed the introductory letter they discussed.

She said, "I'm surprised you missed this!" The letter explained that Mitch would require her expertise and NAJ would be very grateful.

Again, he asked, "Now, who is NAJ again?" She laughed, and reached again into the envelope. "For you being an investigator, you sure miss a lot!"

She took out a second letter, addressed to the Chairman of the Board at Postbank AG, in Bonn, Germany. A personal account had already been set up for Mitch Randolph. The personal letter serve as his introduction.

Mitch grabbed the envelope from her without thinking and said, "I don't get it! Where did all those letters come from? I never saw them before! I don't know *what* is going on here!"

Rachel smiled and said softly, "Sometimes we aren't meant to see everything at one time. Miracles are very seldom explained to us. We just thank God for them."

Then she stood up and turned to Mitch saying,

"Lily and Meagan will be so ecstatic!" Mitch stared at her, bewildered. "How on earth did she know?"

He looked down at the envelope in his hand. Suddenly, he heard a young man say, "How did who know what?" Mitch smiled sheepishly, and said, "I'm sorry. I was just thinking out loud."

The young man had a name tag, Keith Mueller, Supervisor. He smiled back at Mitch and said, "Is someone helping you?"

Mitch replied, "Oh, yeah, Rachel Madison. But we're through now." Keith paused, "Rachel? We have no Rachel working here. All our agents are men!" Mitch dropped down heavily, confused. He hurriedly reached for his envelope. Everything was in order just as she said! But if Rachel wasn't ...*Who* or *whatever was she?*!

A special delivery letter was sent to George Pearson at the school where he taught the nursing class. It was from Mitch Randolph... in Germany. He was reunited with Lily now and they planned the wedding she had always wanted with family, friends, and even 'Oma's' wedding dress.

He wrote in his letter, "George, I'll never forget you, my friend! I wish you the very best. The keys to the cabin are under the seat of my Jeep, so make yourself at home and use the Jeep anytime.

Then Mitch wrote, PS, "I recommended you for the job at the Boys' Home. They can sure use a man like you and the pay is a lot better than you ever got from me!"

George was happy for his friend, but he knew he would always miss Mitch Randolph, the man who taught him self respect.

And what an awesome chance he handed him! He would be a mentor to a group of boys who was not yet bitter nor bruised by an angry world.

God, indeed, had smiled on Forest Hills. And somehow George knew the blessings that were poured down from heaven's window were delivered in part by golden wings and silver letters that spelled NAJ.

Chapter 6 ~ *Edie's Story*

Edie Henson had just finished the lunch shift at the restaurant and her feet were aching. Her tip money was in her pocket but it felt pretty light. The tips were usually good but many regular customers were losing their jobs and she was hearing her tips jingle more as the customers quietly left the diner.

One customer came in just for information and only ordered a cup of coffee. She watched him drive up in that beautiful car of his! Sharon said it was a Lamborghini.

Edie hoped he would order a thick steak and leave a big tip, but all he left was his business card. He said his name was Michael Genucci, with Omega Investments, Ltd. He was looking for a man by the name of Neimann Jackson.

Well, none of us ever heard of him but he was probably one of those out of work guys who stiffed us for a tip. She felt sorry for all of them, though. It wasn't their fault. Just a sign of the times. As the preacher said last month when two more parishioners lost their jobs, "times are hard but we haven't seen anything yet!"

That Sunday, Edie prayed like never before; it was like angels met her at the altar! That day she saw an ad in the Times Journal that gave her hope. Edie was now a single Mom again and she needed a blessing! No, a *miracle* ... just to survive!

Imagine! Someone had a two bedroom house for sale as rent! The payment was lower than her last apartment which only had one bedroom.

As an added incentive, the first payment wasn't due until next month! The owner paid for *all* the legal paperwork and filing fees, too! 'Thank you, NAJ, whoever you are for getting me in this house!'

Pastor Hugh Hayden watched as Edie struggled

to support her son and keep her head above water. Times were hard and working as a waitress didn't offer very much financial security. But Edie was not a complaining woman. She was a *good* woman and a hard worker. He knew she deserved a blessing. If one was looking for a candidate for a house blessing, the pastor was ready to nominate Edie Henson.

She applied to the ad in the Times Journal and his letter of personal reference was included with her application. He prayed and watched, and thanked God for His tender mercies. And then he had the privilege of delivering a letter of acceptance to Edie.

In the upper left-hand corner of the envelope was a stamp, (a pair of angel's wings encircling the letters, NAJ!) But the minister didn't give it a second thought. "Why should you look a gift horse in the mouth?" he thought. "Or ... why doubt a miracle?"

It was like God had an itemized checklist of the woman's needs. There were even some furnishings in the house! With Luke getting out of jail, she needed another bedroom and as if someone read her mind, new bedroom furniture was in the spare room!

Luke Avery was Edie's son. He was a rebellious child... always had been. When Edie and Carl Henson got married, Luke was just seven years old. He took an instant dislike to Carl and refused to accept him as a father. Carl was a building contractor. The year his company got the contract for the new high school being built outside the city limits, he asked Edie to marry him. It was Carl's first marriage.

Edie married Luke's father, Sam Avery, just before Luke was born, so the baby could carry his father's name but she regretted that decision often in the last few years.

Sam Avery was a lady's man. He knew all the single women in town and kept 'knowing' them long after he married Edie. He spent his nights in the local bars and by morning, he was too tired to keep a job.

"What's your ol' lady say about you hangin' out here?" The bartender was Hank Dudley and he knew

Sam was married. But, so were most of the other drunks who came in there every night. Buying drinks for the women at the bar never slowed down the party mood. With their arms around their 'ladies,' one drunk after another passed by ...until they passed out.

"Which old lady are ya talkin' about, Hank?" His words slurred and the bartender guessed he'd be vertical for probably ten minutes more, before he was passed out on the floor and needed to be carried outside where he could sober up.

"Now, Sam, I know you're a married man!" Sam laughed, half choking on his last drink of beer. "No, I ain't married, Hank; she changed *her* name, not me! My lady *here* still needs Sam I am! Come on, woman, it's party time!" One of the barmaids giggled and she hugged him as he slipped her another dollar bill. It probably was one of his wife Edie's bills, from her tip money.

Hank grew tired of the bar scene, but he knew how to tend bar and the money was good. The hours suited him too, because Hank used to be one of the drunks who stayed up all night and slept late every morning. Life was very different in the night. Many relationships were formed and dissolved, influenced by the bottle. Families became fragmented for drunks.

But Hank's life turned around, a little at a time. First, he quit drinking and tried hard to quit smoking. Then Corene Miller came into his life. She was the 'missing link' in his life chain. Suddenly, he had a reason to live and love... and hope.

Corene worked at the Forest Hills Cancer Clinic. Hank's father was in treatment for lung cancer and he drove him to the center. While the disease took its toll on Mr. Dudley, there was someone in the wings, to keep sanity and restore hope and faith. Corene became Hank's one sustaining force.

"Why don't you come to church with me next Sunday?" she asked. Hank shook his head. "Not yet, Miss Miller. The roof would fall in on us if old Hank ever walked through those church doors, an old sinner like me!"

She smiled, "God's in the business of handling 'old sinners like you.' Besides, we just put a new roof on the church so I think you're safe."

Hank didn't feel right about tending bar on a Saturday night and then going to church on Sunday morning. But there was something about Corene that made him dream of possibilities! If God really was watching over him, Corene was probably one of His best angels.

As Hank casually looked across the barroom, he thought, "These guys wouldn't know an angel, if she smacked them in the head with her wings. Old Sam's wife was pretty close to being an angel and look at how he treats her."

Edie was waiting for Sam to get home that night. It was time to talk. Sam had taken all the money she saved for the rent and the baby needed diapers and formula. When he got home, well (what *used to be* his home), she was going to throw him out. She could not afford to pay the bills and take care of the baby on a waitress' salary while he was stealing from her to get drunk! It was time for him to go!

"Six a.m." Edie moaned and looked at the clock. "I have to be at work in an hour! Sam, where are you? Now I have to take the baby to my sister's and I'll be late for work ... again!"

She looked out the window for the umpteenth time and saw no trace of him. She grabbed the diaper bag, a receiving blanket, his favorite toys, and bottles of formula just like all the other times Sam let her down.

Going over the list in her mind, she walked to the front door, muttering, "Car keys! Where are my car keys?" She angrily brushed away her tears. She wasn't going to waste another tear on Sam Avery!

When she opened the door, she saw a young woman with arms crossed, standing by the mailbox watching her.

Edie called to her, "Hello? Are you all right?"

She looked scared and when she uncrossed her arms, Edie thought she would bolt like a frightened deer. Slowly Edie tried to approach her.

"Do I know you? You look familiar." The teenager looked down at her frayed jeans and old, dirty sneakers before she spoke, "You probably know her... my sister, Vera. I mean, you've probably seen her around. We kinda look alike."

Edie watched her and said, "Well, what do you want? Why are you here?" The girl stammered, "Um ... my sister ... uh ... I just wanted you to know, I mean ... I think it's only fair for you to be told ... Oh, God, I hate this! My sister left town today with Sam. I don't even know where they went for sure... I'm sorry ... I really am!"

The girl turned and ran through a neighbor's yard, looking for an escape from her humiliation. She moaned, "Why did they send me to tell that woman her stupid husband was leaving her? Twenty bucks!! If I knew it would be this hard, it would have cost him more, a lot more! Thank God, it's over now."

But for Edie, it was not over. Sam was never a good husband or father, but there was always a little hope that he would change. At least he might have made an attempt to get a job. Now she was truly on her own to raise her son alone. And each year was harder on Edie.

Luke may have sensed her loneliness and fear. Some say that infants can react to a mother's moods. Edie tried hard to make up for Luke's absent father. But even from daycare, the calls came daily:

"Your son has been biting the other children. He's been in time out off and on about all day. He seems to have anger issues. What can we do to help resolve this? If the biting doesn't stop, we'll have no choice but to remove him from our classes."

And it didn't stop until he was enrolled again in the next daycare, where he bullied the other children. He kept hitting and physically attacking the workers.

When Edie met Carl, Luke carried a chip on his

shoulder and it caused many quarrels between them. Edie defended her son, reminding Carl that Luke was abandoned by his father. He tried to convince Edie if she didn't discipline him, one day he would be totally out of control.

When they got married, they made a half-hearted compromise. Carl would keep trying to win Luke over and Edie was determined to keep the problems with Luke's behavior away from Carl.

The Hensons were starting on shakey ground but there were a few good times when Luke would almost be co-operative.

Edie took a few good pictures of Luke and Carl playing basketball in the driveway. She smiled, as she remembered Luke at fifteen, teasing Carl, saying, "Go, Daddy Shaq!" each time he scored, which was a rare event.

Luke, on the other hand, was showing real talent! That year, Carl and Edie celebrated their eighth anniversary and Luke stood between them for the photograph. Edie thought it looked like a real family portrait! It was the summer she would never forget.

Then came the fall and as the clocks were turned back an hour, the evening skies grew dismal and so did any hope of a truce between her husband and her son, Luke. Maybe with time, they would get close. But time was not on their side.

A storm was coming and Carl went to the work site to make sure all the supplies and equipment were covered and battened down. A tornado was spotted in the next county and if he overlooked any precaution, his contract could be in jeopardy.

There was a completion clause, and he only had three weeks to finish or he would face a penalty. If that tornado touched down here his schedule could be thrown off by weeks or months!

Carl fought against the pelting rain, as he ran for the construction site entrance. He grabbed the keys and headed for the main gate leading to his offices. Fumbling with the lock, his fingers felt numb as he tried to get the tumblers to turn in the lock.

Then in the distance he thought he heard a faint sound, like someone calling for help! But the sound of the voice was drowned out by the pelting rain! And that blasted lock would not open! This had to be the right key! Carl could open that entry gate with his eyes closed! Why wouldn't it open now?

He looked up, shielding his face as much as possible from the blinding rain. Someone was yelling! Who could be out here in this storm? And how did he gain entry?

Carl walked around the perimeter fence to a far side of the building where he stored a stack of pallets. He knew he could probably get over the fence there without too much trouble. He would have to climb the stack slowly and then cross over the fence. He made a mental note to move those pallets when this was all over, to keep intruders from entering like he did.

Carl was not a young man anymore. The doctor warned him about his high blood pressure and he was scheduled for a stress test next month.

But Carl wasn't worried. He was healthy as a horse! It was just Edie. She was so concerned for his health! He acted annoyed but if he was being honest, it felt good to know she cared so much.

No, this stack of pallets was nothing to worry about! He'd be in and out in no time. But he knew he had to find out who was inside and why! Obviously, they were in trouble!

But within minutes something had changed; he felt the cold steel as it crashed down on top of him. Darkness engulfed him and he felt himself falling. He could taste his blood and he tried desperately to call out for help...

Yellow tape cordoned off Hinson Construction Company. Police cars with flashing lights blocked the gates at the construction site. There were officers with gloves and evidence bags talking to the coroner.

Questions circulated at the crime scene, "Was it an accident or a homicide? Was anything stolen? Did he have any enemies? Who was the last person to see him alive? Has anyone located the next of kin?"

How could this happen? Carl was always careful. The keys for the equipment were at home locked in his desk. And yet, something happened... the lateral move of the Ferguson crane knocked Carl to the ground. His skull was crushed.

The police report said a switch that prevented the boom on the backhoe from swinging failed to be set by the operator. But no one could find out who was running the backhoe.

No one should have been at the site at night, in a storm, after hours, and especially not alone! The construction equipment would not have been in gear without someone at the controls. But who was it?

Edie stood alone by the grave, covering her face as the tears rolled down her cheeks. She cried out, "God help me. I just don't know how to be by myself again. I can't be alone again, Lord. I tried so hard to be both a father and mother to Luke for many years! Carl and Luke were starting to bond as father and son after all these years. So why must he suffer the loss of yet another father? How can I help him get through this, Lord?"

Edie took a deep breath and tried to compose herself. Again she closed her eyes and spoke to God, "Lord, I need your wisdom and I need your guidance. God, how I thank You for Your saving grace and your mercy! But for today, I need comfort. God, please send me peace enough to face one more day. Amen."

And He watched over her, day by day. Edie went back to her job at the café in September, 1992. She knew it wasn't the best career, but she was a good waitress. Sharon Cox was the owner of the café and she knew Edie kept the customers happy.

She greeted her customers as old friends, like they were VIP guests. And as a result, her tips were always better than any of the other servers'. When other waitresses groaned about tips and wages, Edie said, 'At least it pays the bills.' She knew how scarce work was, and she felt blessed to have her job. She learned early in life that God sends opportunities and hard work to set the stage for answered prayer and miracles.

Sharon was quick to recognize Edie's potential so when she came back to work at the cafe, she was promoted as the manager (with server duties).

She smiled as she remembered the proud look on Sharon's face, when she told her she would see a *big* change in her paycheck since her '*promotion.*'

On Friday, the bank cashed her biggest check she ever earned at the café; twenty dollars was the pay raise that Sharon gave her so proudly!

Sarcastically, she thought, 'A whole twenty bucks for such *menial* tasks as budgeting, ordering supplies, cooking, employee shift scheduling, assigning jobs, and bussing all the tables, housekeeping, and keeping up with all receipts!'

But to be fair, she didn't mind. The café was a second home to her. She loved everything about her job. Edie counted her tips for the day, $27.13. Then she smiled, wondering who it was that left the thirteen cents. Maybe it was all he had left. "Well, I thank God for thirteen cents, that's all I have to say!"

Edie walked into the bedroom she prepared for Luke. He was going to be released from jail today. He was always in some kind of trouble. Now, maybe he would see the way God was blessing them and try harder to stay out of trouble.

Luke said the police just 'had it in for him' because he had a record. They treated Luke like he was guilty before they ever heard anything from him. Even Edie saw that. But in all fairness, she knew he earned his poor reputation by breaking the law.

This time he was in jail for assault. The woman claimed he hit her and broke her jaw. Luke denied it but his fist was injured that night and the victim's neighbors claimed to have seen them arguing before the police were called.

Edie tried to ask Luke what happened, wanting

so badly to believe her son was innocent. But her questions made him angry and he accused her of never trusting him. "Maybe if you would have ever given me the benefit of a doubt, just maybe you wouldn't be seeing your kid in jail now! You're not without blame, you know!"

Edie left him at the visitation room at the jail, and never came back until he called her collect and told her to come and pick him up on his release date. She prayed before she started the car, "God, it would be just great if You sent my son home with a better attitude."

The county jail was coming into view and a lone figure stood impatiently waiting just inside the chain linked fence. The barb wire at the top of the twelve foot security fence was placed there specifically to keep in dangerous prisoners so they would not escape.

It brought tears to her eyes. This was her son! But the man she saw standing there inside the prison gate was the image of a dangerous criminal. How ironic that her tiny baby boy was born July 4th, 1976, as the fireworks were set off, bombarding the skies, while families across America celebrated freedom. Now, here he stood behind prison walls with barb wire to keep the public safe from him.

Something inside told her to run! But there was also the mother inside her heart who drove quickly to the guard's booth to retrieve her son.

After presenting the required identification, she was frisked by a female guard, who searched her for weapons or contraband. Her keys and purse were held at the first guards' station.

She was then led into a room where she was asked to wait while he completed his 'transitioning.' Edie asked her, "What is this 'transitioning' they said they were doing? I don't think I've ever heard of that before!"

The woman never smiled, but she explained, "It's a new program through the prison system to help the inmate. If he 'transitions' or to changes his attitude and lifestyle as he re-enters an unrestrained life, it will help him to improve his self discipline with others in society." ("Lord, if only that would work for Luke," she prayed aloud).

Soon she saw Luke walking towards her. She cautiously offered him a slight smile of encouragement. But there was no trace of any love or even gratitude from Luke. "Get me out of here," he demanded.

Edie tried to understand her son's anger. Maybe he was ashamed to be in jail; or maybe he was mad at her for not visiting him while he was incarcerated. No, he was probably just under a great deal of stress going through all the red tape required for his release. After a good night's sleep, he could relax. Tomorrow would be a much better day.

Edie positioned the driver's seat and adjusted her mirrors. She had almost convinced herself that Luke was glad to be coming home ... almost.

This year, 2001, may be the year of promise as well as a blessing! After all, Edie Henson held the keys to a new home! Thank God! And bless NAJ, whoever you are!

Edie received another linen envelope the week after Luke was released; gold wings encircled NAJ as before. She had unlocked the door to her new home in Rose Court. She dropped into the chair, exhausted from her long shift at the diner. She kicked off her shoes before she began to read the contents of her letter, written as if it were poetry:

"A family consists of tears, needs, laughter and joy. Life, not birth, shall always be the key-note of true family entitlement. Memories are an inheritance of that union. Open your heart, my Daughter, and be loved once more."

But the troubled son *she* loved was 'once more' arrested. He was released from prison and within days he was behind bars again. This time, he was accused of murder. And they had a full confession.

She walked into 'Luke's room,' but Luke was no longer there. She thought of her son, now heading for

Death Row for taking two lives.

"Be loved?" she thought. "I have no one *left* to love me," she said, as the telephone rang for the fifth time. She grabbed it impatiently. "Edie Henson!" Luke always hated that she never answered the telephone with the usual 'hello.'

The caller was Vicky from the café. "We might have a big problem with a customer, Edie, and I'd feel better if you were here."

Edie rubbed her temples and said, "Vicky, I don't understand, Hon. What kind of problem? Talk to me, Vicky. Can't you deal with it without me?"

She was a new waitress and Edie was trying to encourage her. She would make a good waitress some day, but the least little thing could cause her to panic.

"I think you just better come in." Edie began to get annoyed and nothing annoyed Edie. "Vicky, you aren't making any sense... oh, never mind, I'll be right there." She murmured, "I need the distraction now, anyways. I was about to lose my mind sitting here."

As Edie pulled into her parking space, she saw there were no customers parked out in front. 'Is it possible they decided to leave?' she thought. As she walked to the cafe door, Vicky came out on the porch to meet her. "What's wrong, Vicky? And where is the 'unhappy' customer?"

Vicky turned her back to the window and kept her voice low. "A couple of hours ago, a young man came in with an elderly couple. I thought they were his grandparents!" As Vicky continue with her story, her voice started to tremble, "But Edie, he hit him! He hit that poor old man!"

Edie stopped her suddenly, "Whoa, Girl! *Who* hit the poor old man?" Edie shook her head to clear her thoughts. "You need to sit down and tell me the whole story, but you can't skip around, Vicky! You're just confusing me!"

The young waitress started again, "I'm so sorry, Edie. I know you said to be nice to customers but I was not to interfere with their privacy.

So when this party of three entered, I seated them, saying, 'Good evening.' The old woman said, 'Oh, Dear! I think they're closing, she's saying good night to us.' I thought she was adorable. The older gentleman gently said, 'No, Dear, she's just greeting us. If it were morning, she would have said, 'Good Morning.' Now... do you understand?' "

Edie could easily picture the two of them, like her elderly aunt and uncle who raised her. She smiled remembering them.

"Well, the young man got so mad! He told them to 'go sit down and shut up!' Then he shoved the old guy into the chair. I was trying to mind my business, I really was! But he sure was making me mad!"

Edie could imagine Vicky having a temper. She had the fiery red hair but a heart of gold. She told her to go on with the story. "Well, *Sonny* decided to order a *steak* for himself and just a bowl of *soup* for the old couple. Then he said, "And you better not make a mess if you know what's good for you!"

Vicky's face was red hot relating the incident to Edie. "Well, to make a long story short, the poor old woman knocked over her water glass, then the old man jumped up to help her. He *spilled his soup*... so then..." she hung her head, "he cussed them both out and started shoving them around."

Edie knew there was more to the story by the way Vicky's voice got a little quieter. "Go on." The younger waitress bit her lip and said, "I... I told him to knock it off and to pick on someone his own size."

Edie arched her eyebrow, "And *he* said...?" The young woman's voice quivered, " For me to mind my own business or he'd give me a lesson himself."

Edie was really angry. "And where is Mr. Wonderful now?" Vicky looked up sheepishly, and said, "Wait, Edie ... there's more. I sort of snatched him out of his chair and threw him out the door. So he's... gone."

Edie looked at her wide-eyed, "You did what?!" Vicky shrugged, and her voice became defensive "Hey,

I got six older brothers!" Her voice got weaker when she explained, "I reacted without thinking it through, Edie! I hope I didn't get the diner in any trouble. I'm so sorry."

"Sorry?! You could have been killed!!" Edie was appalled! She asked Vicky, "Are you okay? Do you need to see a doctor or anything?" Vicky quickly assured her employer, "I'm fine, do *not* be worried about me! I'm the least of your problems!"

Edie stepped back and took a deep breath. She eyed Vicky closely, saying, "Wow... but it's over, right?" Slowly, the young waitress said, "Well, as they say, 'now here's the rest of the story,'" She walked into the café ahead of Edie. "He's gone ... they're not."

Sitting at the corner table was Elmer and Eleanor Scofield. Edie did *not* believe in reincarnation but the old man *looked* like Uncle Reese! He wore the same round glasses, rosy cheeks and a smile like a cherub.

And if that wasn't enough of a shock, Eleanor was dainty in her navy and white print housedress, her gray hair tightly permed and she wore just a hint of lipstick to accent the little smile she wore, just like Aunt Bessie!

"Oh, no... I must be dreaming. This can't be real. I have to sit down," Edie said, feeling weak. This was unbelievable! Clara, the other server came to her rescue, calling to Vicky, "Bring me a damp washcloth! And get her a glass of water!"

Edie needed to close her eyes for just a second. But then when she opened her eyes, Eleanor Scofield was wiping her face, "Are you all right, Dear? You gave us quite a scare!"

She bolted upright suddenly and looking around the café, she saw Elmer bringing her a cup of tea! Edie recovered and was told the story of the Scofield's plight. The man who brought them to the café was Louie Bell, a paid caregiver, with the heart of a viper!

He took both their retirement checks and only fed them when and how he chose. The elderly couple had been abused and neglected but they were helpless!

They tried to help each other so he wouldn't get so angry.

Edie wanted the police called but they were afraid Louie *would* be brought back. "But where will we go, Dear? Mr. Louie's house is where we live now. He has all our clothes and he still has our medicine, too! Oh, Elmer, I am so afraid!"

The fragile woman's broken heart touched Edie Henson's spirit. She watched as Elmer reached out to his wife. He was trying to comfort her, but he felt inadequate as a husband, believing he let her down somehow having no solutions to ease her fears.

"Now, Eleanor, don't be afraid, Sweetheart. I'll figure something out. I've always taken care of us for the past sixty years, haven't I?"

She smiled weakly, nodding. "Yes, Dear, you have always been a good husband. But now we are old and our home is gone..." Elmer sadly tried to comfort his wife. "Will you please trust me, Eleanor? I promise I will do something."

Edie remembered the letter she received and suddenly everything began to make sense. She stood up, and spoke to the elderly couple. "Wait a minute! I've got the answer but it may sound a little crazy at first. You see, I have a brand new home and I live alone. You can move in with me! It won't cost you a cent! You would have a bedroom with a private bath and you can even fix up your room any way you want. How does that sound to you?"

Elmer looked stunned. "How could we impose on you like that? We have nothing to offer you in return. Why would you want to do this for us? We aren't even family!"

Edie smiled, "I remembered something someone told me recently, 'A family consists of tears and needs, joy and laughter.' I was reminded it is *life* and not *birth* that entitles one to a family's love.

Eleanor Scofield brushed away a tear as she said, "You must have been sent to us from heaven, dear. God never saw fit to bless our home with children, although Elmer would have been a wonderful father.

Our infant daughter was stillborn and I never recovered from losing her. My heart and my arms have ached to hold my daughter. We have so much love to give. But Elmer and I have been alone for years, simply taking care of each other! And thank God we had each other!"

Edie put her arms around the Scofields and held them close. "So as of this moment, *Uncle* Elmer and *Aunt* Eleanor, you are now *my* family. Welcome home!"

Edie thanked God for answered prayer, divine intervention and a messenger known by golden wings encircling three silver letters... NAJ.

Chapter 7 ~ *Daryl's Story*

Across the driveway from the cemetery entrance, a driver was sitting patiently, waiting for his passenger to return.

Daryl was an experienced driver and he assumed full responsibility for the maintenance and repairs on the old Lincoln Town Car. Hardly any maintenance was required, since the automobile had only 10,000 miles on it!

The man was easy to work for, too. It seemed he rarely spoke, unless he was asking for a favor from God. He seemed to be constantly planning, calculating, and figuring so it was quite apparent that he wanted no idle chatter, which suited Daryl just fine. He was a private person, as well.

Daryl watched his passenger approach the car. He opened the rear passenger door, and returned to his seat behind the wheel to wait for his rider to seat himself.

His employer established the ground rules with him on the very first day, "I am acquainted personally with just *one* King and I am His servant. If you want to open my door, it will be at your discretion. But I will *always* close it... at *my* discretion." Daryl replied, "Yes, sir. I understand."

The old man smiled as he closed his car door. The driver glanced in the rear view mirror, and saw the old man close his eyes as he began to pray to God ... again.

He slowly drove away from the cemetery, where they had been placing flowers on several graves since 6 a.m. Now Daryl was told to drive him to the north side of town. He slowed the car down as he entered the city limits.

The sun was faintly casting the rays of morning through the treetops and traces of snow were reflecting on the banks along the roadside.

He loved the early morning in Forest Hills. It was a beautiful time of day for memories. Daryl brushed off a tear as he remembered the fishing trips he and his dad shared before he died. Oscar Baker loved to fish more than anyone he ever knew!

But suddenly the sun broke through, and the new dawn renewed the memories he tried to forget, the months spent back in Nam. Fear had a way of setting priorities in order. Life became more precious and the blessings of God were seen in a whole new light.

Daryl smiled as he heard his passenger speak. He heard the old man talking to Someone as though they were in the seat next to him, "Father, may Your will be done and may Your humble servant be blessed with the grace to do Your bidding."

Daryl kept silent but thought, 'He sure loves the Lord, but he has to be the strangest man I ever met.' It was hard to believe he had been driving the old man for these past several years. But his life turned around soon after he met the old man.

Daryl was a Vietnam veteran, deployed in 1969. He was one of the last soldiers who left the country in February of 1973, but not before he met Victor-Charlie, (the Viet Cong) face to face.

And the next thing he knew he was getting his head bandaged by a beautiful nurse. He just knew she had to be beautiful; her voice was like an angel's song. But the soldier had no sight. His brain injuries were major. The high velocity bullets penetrated his brain, and perferated his spine. He was paralyzed and blind, but he thanked God for his life.

The angel who took care of him was with the 95th Evacuation Hospital. It was the last one to close with the mass exodus of American soldiers in March.

He couldn't forget the gentle touch of the angel's hands, but he was an honorable man with a fiancé back home waiting for his return. At least he thought he did.

Soon after he arrived stateside, his family was

told he would be coming home in a matter of days. He was escorted from the aircraft by the medical personnel. He was still sightless, but he didn't need sight to see that something was wrong. He felt tension in the air.

He raised his hand to motion the medical escort to stop. He listened closely for the sound of her voice, but it never came; Cheryl "CeeCee" Carver was not there to greet his plane. It seemed that she was too busy making other plans ... with her *husband and a baby girl*!

All those days and nights, he dreamed of getting married. He could even imagine the babies they would have together. But while he was there in Vietnam in the trenches fighting for her freedom, she was going on with her life as if he had died.

She should have been honest enough to break up with him right away. Many of the GI's got 'Dear John' letters, and she could have told him. But then Daryl remembered the day when ol' 'Dude' Mackenzie received his DJ from his wife. He never said a word. He just marched out onto the field, pulled the pin on the grenade, and fell to the ground screaming, as he clutched it to his chest. Maybe Cee Cee did the right thing after all.

But one thing was certain in his mind, if he had known, the angel at the 95th would have received more than a 'thank you, ma'am!' But he resigned himself to the fact that he would never meet her again. He just had his memories to make him smile.

If he closed his eyes, he could once more feel the touch of her hands massaging his temples. He heard her laughter and for just a second, there was a hint of her perfume in the air. He wiped away the tear from the corners of his sightless eyes.

He dropped his hand into his lap and hung his head. The medical escort placed a comforting hand on his shoulder and said, "Sir, there appears to be a lady at the door of the terminal waving a handkerchief. And I believe she is calling your name."

Daryl smiled. It was the handkerchief that gave her away. Mama had to travel quite a distance to bring him home. He turned his head and listened, and smiled.

"Daryl! I am here, son! I'm over here, can you hear me?" Daryl burst into laughter, "Yes, Mama, I hear you! The whole east coast can hear you!"

In his mind's eye, he could just imagine seeing her wave that little, flowery handkerchief! It was her own 'claim to fame,' as the preacher used to say. As the hymns were blessing her, Mama Baker would get out her handkerchief, tearfully waving it in the air as she cried out, "Hallelujah, Jesus, hallelujah!"

Matilda Baker loved her little Forest Hills Church of Faith and her pastor, Hugh Hayden. But recently, her heart was failing her so she wasn't able to attend as often as she would have liked.

When Oscar Baker, Daryl's father, died in March, 1969, Matilda was ready to give up on life. She was soon hospitalized and even spent time in hospice when her recovery looked doubtful.

While she was a patient there she met a man who came and prayed with her and held her hand when she mourned for Oscar. It was like they were acquaintances for a lifetime! They became the best of friends and for the next few years, Matilda Baker grew strong. She was happy to be active in church again. Her banana nut bread was a favorite in the church suppers.

Daryl was reluctant about going off to war, but it was something he felt he had to do for his country. "If only I could be sure Mama would be all right till I get back," he said to her friend.

The old man reached out and touched Daryl's hand, then gripped it firmly, saying, "My friend, you need not be concerned about Tilly. She is in my very capable hands. I will tend to Mama. You must go and serve your country but return safely. I pray for God's grace and blessings upon you, Daryl Baker."

And with that promise held close to his heart,

he went to Vietnam to fight a war nobody wanted and nobody won. Now Mama was waving her flowery handkerchief. There standing next to her was the old man who promised to look after her, which he did admirably.

Daryl was admitted to the VA hospital close to home. He had two surgical procedures on his eyes before he regained any sight but his vision was greatly impaired. Slowly, he was beginning to heal physically, following months of rehab. But the doctors were concerned about his depression; they told him he was experiencing post traumatic stress syndrome, from being in the war.

But now, he prayed that God would help him find a job to be able to provide for his mother and not be a burden to her. After Oscar died, Matilda moved to a less expensive apartment in town.

He returned to the states in 1974 after spending a few months in an army hospital in Germany. For the next five years, he was in and out of surgical centers, hospitals, and rehab centers until they had almost pieced him back together.

It seemed like everyone in Forest Hills knew Daryl or 'about' Daryl. The rumors and gossip were rampant, "He's that boy who got hurt in the war." "That's the Bakers' son, crippled from a land mine!" "Daryl's the one who came back from Nam with his head all messed up." "He had a nervous breakdown or something after the war, didn't he?"

Everyone had a preconceived notion of what was wrong with him, but no one was willing to hire him. His veteran's benefits were practically an insult to a soldier who offered his life for his country. And for several years, the jobs he was offered or was capable of doing were few and far between.

Suddenly, his mother's old friend was there to offer him a job as his driver. Daryl was overcome with emotion as he shook the old man's hand, sealing the deal...ten years ago. He would be forever thankful.

There were never lengthy chats with the old man,

but each time he was summoned as his driver, he was prepared for the long, prayerful talks he had *with God*, while riding in the back seat alone.

Daryl appreciated the privilege of driving the old man's car for him. A more beautiful vehicle was not to be found anywhere. The 1985 Lincoln Town Car was a deep midnight blue and could have just been driven off the showroom floor! He was proud to be the driver.

The seats were real leather. The interior was as white as snow and there was not a spot of dirt or a sign of wear and tear. A red buzzer had been installed where the cigarette lighter was originally located, so he could signal Daryl if needed, while he was driving. An electric privacy window was also installed when it was purchased but Daryl was never asked to close it.

He enjoyed listening to the way he talked to God while they were driving through the country. But lately, there had been so much tragedy in Forest Hills, the old man seemed to be walking slower and praying more.

At times, Daryl caught himself praying for the old man. He hated to think something might happen to him. No one seemed to know his age but he was smart! And nothing got past that old man!

Daryl faked a cough to hide the chuckle that escaped when he remembered the time when someone tried to con him out of five dollars. The money was not the issue for the old man, but a lesson was taught to the beggar and Daryl, too!

A man in his mid twenties tapped on the window and leaned in to asked if he had five dollars he was able to spare. The old man opened his window and greeted the younger man in a cordial manner, "Good morning, sir! Isn't this a beautiful day the Lord has made for us?" The younger man said, "Uh, yeah, I guess it is at that."

He wanted to ask for the money right away but the old man said quickly, " You should always thank God for three things, young man, your health, your strength, and opportunity! And in return, He will supply every need you may have. So what was it you wanted from me?"

The beggar stood up straight and said, "Uh, I just, well... God bless you, sir. Have a nice day." The old man smiled and said, "It's been a pleasure to meet you, Rick." Then the window went up and they drove away. Daryl wondered how the old man knew the beggar's name!

As they approached the old Sinclair station on the corner of Main Street and Coulter Avenue, he told Daryl to pull into the station. He told him, "Sir, the fuel tank is full. Why are we stopping?" He said, "I just needed to have a word with the young officer over there." Daryl looked around in all directions and there was no officer nor cruiser in sight. In fact, even the service station looked closed!

Then out of nowhere, a trooper approached their car, smiling. The old man greeted him and handed an envelope to him with the angel wings in the left hand corner, encircling the letters NAJ. The officer opened it and nodded. Daryl looked past him and saw lights in the station! And someone was inside looking out the window!!

Daryl heard the old man say, "Take him over to Miller's Bed and Breakfast. Corene has been trying to make a go of her parents' old hotel but ever since she lost her job at the cancer clinic, she hasn't been able to afford to keep it open.

That should pay for the young man's keep for a month or so." The officer smiled and said, "I'm sure Corene will appreciate the business, too." Then the old man gave him a second envelope.

"And could you please deliver this to Hudson's Hardware down on Main Street? It should take care of all the tools and supplies that Rick will need to help get their inn back in shape."

The policeman touched the bill of his hat and said, "Will do, sir!" Daryl kept silent while all the plans were being made. Then the 'buzz' sounded and

Daryl responded, "Yes, sir?" He turned to see which direction the police cruiser turned, but it was nowhere in sight.

"Please take us back to the highway, Daryl." The driver looked again, both directions, but there was no sign of the police car and the station appeared to be abandoned and boarded up!

'What just happened here?' Daryl directed his attention to the road. At least driving was something he could make sense out of.

As he made the right turn and headed through the outskirts of town, he saw a faded sign that said, "Miller's Bed and Breakfast" and the next sign said, "Under New Management ~ Corene Miller Dudley, Mgr." The signpost was broken and the sign was held in place by a rusty nail! The whole place seemed to be boarded up, with no plans to reopen!

Daryl started worrying, 'maybe the old man was starting to show signs of mental stress. No one knew how old he was and sometimes old folks did start acting strange when they got a certain age, right?'

But all the rationalizing didn't change the fact that he spoke to an officer, (who disappeared), at a gas station (that was out of business), and funded the restoration of a Bed and Breakfast, (that was boarded up). But other than that, the day was going just great! 'Lord, help us... please!'

The old man seemed to be napping so Daryl was careful not to disturb him. He decided to pull off the road at a small truck stop to get a hot cup of coffee. The faded sign in the window said they also served beer on tap. But Daryl quit drinking years ago.

"Lord, tell me this was not a test." With all the weird things he witnessed a few miles back, if he *were* still a drinking man, he would have had a *real* good excuse.

Daryl looked back at the old man who was beginning to stir. "Is everything all right, Daryl?" He told him, "Yes, sir, I just thought I would stop for a cup of coffee. Is there anything you would like while I'm in there?"

He shook his head, "No, just take your time, son. But you *could* tell Hank that Rick might need his help this afternoon at the inn. I think I'm going to take a little nap while you're enjoying your coffee."

Daryl cautiously responded; the old man was probably just tired, so he repeated, "Tell Hank... Rick... Sure, sure! You just relax. I'll be right back."

He slowly opened the door of the restaurant and glanced at the red stools at the counter. The tables were picnic benches covered with red vinyl tablecloths.

He walked to the stool closest to the register and leaned on the counter. He could smell the aroma of fresh coffee brewing but he saw no one available to take his order.

"Hello! Is there anybody here? Are you open for business?" Daryl walked back to the door and tugged on the bell that announced someone had just entered.

A man in his fifties came out of the back room carrying an order pad. "Sorry, Fella. I didn't mean to keep you waiting. I guess I just can *not* get the hang of this waitressing... waitering or whatever you want to call it." Daryl liked him right away. He knew the man was embarrassed but he just laughed it off, "Ok, order whenever you're ready, sir."

Daryl said, "Uh, yeah, I guess I just want a small coffee to go." He hesitated before saying, " I know this is probably going to sound a little crazy, but by any chance, would your name be Hank?

The man laid down his order pad, and eyed him suspiciously. "Who wants to know?" Daryl laughed, "No... there's no problem. My friend just wanted me to leave a message with Hank. I just wondered if you were Hank."

Daryl watched the waiter lean against the wall and breath a sigh of relief. "You had me worried for a minute. Yeah, I'm Hank. I guess I'm just a bit gunshy. This place used to be a bar years ago. I was the bartender. It was a little on the wild side. Then I met an angel.

But, hey, let me get your coffee. You probably ain't got time to be listening to my babblin!" Daryl slowly shook his head. "No, believe me, I got time. After a day like I've had, I got all the time in the world." He could be friends with Hank. He was easy to talk to.

"Okay! Well, here's your cup of Java. It's on the house. You see, my old man, I mean, my father... he died of cancer a while back. But while he was going for his treatments, I met a Christian lady, (her name's Corene). I was a bartender when she asked me to go to church with her. Crazy, huh?"

Daryl shrugged and continued. "Well, she started prayin' and I guess I was talking to God about it, too. Then, BAM! The bar shuts down! The owners were leavin' town! I was without a job! Man, I was ticked off! I never expected God to put me out of my job! I had bills to pay! I had a little cash put back, you know, for a rainy day ... but not for this!"

He shook his head. "So Corene told me to talk to her preacher, Pastor Hayden. Well, we talked and he prayed for us. And out of the clear blue sky, the guy who owned the bar comes and asks me if I want to buy it! I *always* wanted to have my own place, but now just how would that look?

I'm prayin,' the preacher's prayin' and Corene's prayin' that God would help me solve my employment problem. Then the *bar* is offered to me. Could I really *own* a bar that I used to work at? It already got me nervous about going to church the morning after *selling* men alcohol the night before.

What a sorry predicament I found myself in!" Hank raised both hands in frustration. "But guess what... the preacher came to my house with an odd letter. Inside the envelope was a little book that some-one had printed. It was about a couple converting a tavern into a cozy bed and breakfast somewhere in Vermont. Then there were pamphlets on how to open and run a small roadside restaurant, truck stop or diner." Hank smiled as he told his story.

"Just about that time I complained that this had been a bar for so long, it would probably be a long time before I could see a profit. Then the pastor said, 'How long? A month? A year? What if you had the financial backing to keep you afloat for a year? Then could you make it work?'

Me and my big mouth! I said, 'Yeah, but I *don't* have that kind of backing, so it doesn't really matter all that much!' " He chuckled as he thought of that day, and remembered the conversation.

"Well, the preacher man smiled and pulled out a check from the envelope and said, "Well, now you do!" My jaw dropped! Then, when I fully recovered, I went to the bank, signed the papers and opened Dudley's Truck Stop. Now, whaddya think? Have you ever heard anything so odd?"

Daryl was sitting on a red stool, resting his arms on the counter. He smiled, shaking his head. Turning to Hank, he said, "Hey, I saw a 'Beer On Tap' sign in the window. It sure brought me back to the day when I downed a few!"

Hank hung his head, "I guess I need to take it down. I don't serve alcohol now; it just reminds me how far I came. It's been weird, Man!"

Daryl nodded, "Why don't you add this to your weird experiences? I have a message for you. Rick will need you to help him at Corene's Bed and Breakfast tonight. He's picking up his supplies and then starting to work on the inn tomorrow." Hank stood back and stared at Daryl.

"You know my wife? Who is Rick? The bed and breakfast is closed! It's...well, it's in *bad* shape. How do you know all this?" Daryl shook his head and said, "Don't ask! Just go with it and don't be late. I don't know for sure how reliable Rick will be."

Daryl stood up and zipped his jacket. "Well, good talkin' to ya, Hank... and thanks for the coffee!" Daryl walked out to the parking lot and opened the driver's door of the Lincoln. The old man was covered up with the blanket he kept in the back seat.

"Daryl, is everything all right, son?" He smiled, "Yes, sir, everything is great." He paused before he turned the key in the ignition, reflecting on the past years he worked for the old man.

He took a flight to Nevada for him once, and several times he drove his employer to the airport for a trip overseas where he had to take care of business. Yet he never once drove him to an office or his home. Daryl parked the Lincoln in a garage next to his own apartment building after each day's travel. He always met his employer at the corner by the Forest Hills Church of Faith.

He knew it was his respect for the man's privacy that kept his job secure, so he pushed aside all the questions out of his mind. He checked his rear mirror and asked, "Where to, sir?" The old man was smiling, "Let's stop by the Pleasant Grove Hospital, Daryl."

The driver looked back worried, "Are you all right, sir? You're not ill, are you? Should I take you to the emergency entrance?" The old man laughed, "Relax, son, I am fine. But you *will* need to enter at the pediatrics center, on the right after the turning lane up ahead."

Daryl followed the directions without question and parked in a space next to the door. That was another oddity! Every time the Lincoln entered a parking lot, the best space opened for them. Coincidence? It could be, but what a coincidence!

As Daryl stopped the car, the old man stepped out and asked him to walk across the street to the florist shop and pick up the red, long stemmed roses he had ordered.

Daryl asked him, "Whom shall I say ordered the flowers, sir?" The man kept walking to the hospital entrance, but casually turned slightly to Daryl and smiled. "You won't be asked for any information."

Daryl knew without a doubt the old man would be right, but how did he know? He entered the shop and the flower arrangements and balloons made him forget it was the Christmas season. He remembered

-112-

the time he was flown into Hawaii when he was a soldier. At first, the memories made him smile until his memories carried him back to Nam with dead bodies on the fields of war. He choked back tears as he walked to the sales' counter.

"Excuse me, Ma'am, but I've been sent to pick up roses that had been ordered..." Without hesitating, the young girl smiled and said, "She's one lucky lady." and handed him the roses, no questions asked, just as the old man had promised.

Daryl walked back to wait for his employer at the Lincoln and he placed the roses on the front seat beside him. 'Roses... there was something about roses he was trying to remember. Suddenly, the words were almost shouted to him from his past, 'How could you forget? That nurse *angel,* from the 95th Evacuation Hospital said she was waiting for Mr. Right to come sweep her off her feet.

Daryl remembered asking, "How will you know if he's *Mr. Right* and *not Bubba* Wrong!" She laughed. (What a great laugh she had!) "Because my man will be carrying a full dozen long stemmed roses!" Daryl smiled remembering how she cheered him up that day.

He laughed, wondering just how many men would be walking around with long stemmed roses. Not too many, that's for sure. And especially not in Nam!

The old man came out of the hospital and stood motioning to him. "Daryl, come! And bring the roses, please." He picked up the flowers and hurried to his employer.

"Daryl, please carry the flowers to Room 279 on the second floor. Then you will be free to do whatever you like. I won't need you to drive me back. I will call you in the morning. God go with you."

He turned, reentering the hospital lobby. Daryl followed just a few steps behind the old man. As he touched the closing entry door, he saw the atrium and corridors... but the old man, who entered just seconds ahead of him, was not to be found! Daryl thought, 'He can sure move quickly for an old man!'

He proceeded to the elevator that would carry him to Room 279. As the elevator doors opened, he noticed how many women smiled, seeing the roses. He wondered, 'How many of those women do you think have even received one rose from the love of their life in the past year?'

After hearing his 'angel' nurse in Nam say how important it was for her to receive her roses, Daryl made up his mind that his wife, (whoever she may turn out to be), would never lack flowers, nor love.

"277, 281... 281? 279 was missing! That can't be right!!" Again he retraced his steps. "275, 277, 281!" The nurse at the Attendant's Center Desk chuckled as she pretended not to notice his frustration.

Finally, he walked to the desk where the nurse had turned around to hide her amusement. "Ahem, excuse me." She ignored his presence. "Ma'am? Hello there! Ahem!" She turned to face him with a guilty smile on her face. He grinned back at her and said, "I do believe you were *enjoying* my dumb floundering! *Shame* on you!"

The young attendant was smiling at him. "My name is Daryl Baker, and for some reason, I've been sent to Room 279, which doesn't seem to exist. Am I right? Or just plain blind?" She laughed then, while apologizing, "I'm sorry, sir, but if you only knew how many times I've had to explain the room numbers on this floor!"

She stepped away from her desk and stood next to him. Then she pointed in the direction of the elevators and said, "Room 279 is right there." He looked around and then looked back at the nurse, "You are kidding, right?"

The numbers were hung like signposts beside all the rooms and not one read 279. She walked down the hall and motioned for him to follow. She said, "No, I'm not kidding. I said, Room 279 is right there but you just don't follow directions very well, do you, Daryl Baker?"

Suddenly Daryl saw a door open and an older

nurse stepped into the hallway. "Maxi, if you are pulling your pranks again, you are in big trouble, girl!"

The young nurse laughed, "I'm sorry, Nicole, but it's just that some people are so gullible, I can't resist! It's so boring here on the late shift! I was just having some fun. Sorry, sir. Here is Room 279, in the *right* inset beside Room 277, just like it's supposed to be. And *this* bossy lady is Nicole!

I swear, Nicky, you should have just stayed in the army! As a drill sergeant and not a nurse! 'Cause you have NO sense of humor!"

The older nurse acted angry and swatted at her playfully with the paperwork she held in her hand. "I'm sorry, sir, you shouldn't have to deal with our foolishness. Obviously, Maxi wasn't helping you so now what can I do for you?"

Daryl stopped and took a couple of steps back, and read the sign on the glass door showing number 279. *"Post-Op Care and Rehabilitation."* Daryl asked, "Is this your office?" She laughed, and wondered if he would ever trust a nurse again. "Yes, sir, this is my office, I swear!"

Daryl nearly dropped the roses when he heard the sound of her laughter. He started to stutter, "I know you! No, I ... I mean I *knew* you! I *think* I knew you! No! I mean, it's *really* you! My *angel!*"

She warily took a step back, to make some sense out of his outburst. "I am sorry, but I have no idea what you are talking about!" He took a deep breath as he gazed into the bluest eyes he had ever seen! Even after all these years, she was still beautiful! He knew she would be!

He laid down the box of roses and reached for her hand. "Vietnam ... February, 1973. You were the nurse with the 95th Evacuation Hospital. So please tell me you haven't forgotten me! I'm Daryl Baker! I was blind and paralyzed but now..." He released her hand and stopped when he saw her crying.

She said, "You went home to Cheryl. Of course, I remember you and for years I cried each time I had to think of you with her. You always carried a picture of her everywhere!"

Daryl shook his head, "No! You don't understand! I came home feeling guilty for my feelings I had for you, but I couldn't be unfaithful to her." She nodded, "I do understand."

Again, he shook his head, "No, you don't understand... Cheryl *wasn't* waiting for me when I returned from Nam. She got married the month after I had shipped out and had his baby before I got home! I was never told!"

Nicole was shocked and angry. "Do you mean... you were risking your life in that God-awful war zone, and she cheated on you? She married someone else? How could she do that to you? I'd like to give her a piece of my mind!" Daryl shook his head. He just couldn't take his eyes off her!

"None of that matters anymore, Nicole! I kept praying to God that He would bring you back to me. If I would have known she was not home waiting for me, I could have told you back then I loved you! I have always loved you! Even when I was blind, your voice kept me alive! I knew you were my angel. Just your touch on my fevered brow, gave me strength!"

Nicole started crying again and Daryl got scared, "Oh, no! Oh, God, don't let it be! You got married, didn't you? How foolish of me to think you just lived in limbo."

Nicole laughed, "No! I'm not married! I never got married! I couldn't! I always loved you and only you!" He held her close but when he looked past her at her desk, he saw a picture of two smiling little girls.

He asked slowly, "Are they yours?" She laughed, "Oh, yeah, they're mine all right! The one on the right is Thien, meaning *'heavenly'* and Tuyen, which means *'angel'*, is on the left. I adopted them when I figured I would never have my own children. My heart was left in Vietnam and they were orphans so I wanted to bring them here to America. If it wasn't for someone from NAJ, I probably could never have managed it."

Daryl held his breath, "Did you say, NAJ?" She nodded. "I think it is some kind of organization that helps with Asian adoptions. I'm not sure about all the details.

But I was I was just about to give up hope when a letter was sent to me in an odd envelope. I know it had a cottony texture like currency, like paper money! In the upper left-hand corner, were golden wings and silver letters that said NAJ. Inside were legal papers that permitted my children to leave Viet Nam... to come to America!

I was directed to come to Virginia where I was taught their culture. Then after three months, my girls arrived, they received grief counseling and I became a 'Meh'. It's how they say Mommy.

I was offered this job so we stayed on. I bought a house in Rose Court and we became a real family! NAJ even helped me find my home at a *great* price! I don't really know who they are, but I include them in my prayers every night!"

Daryl was still holding her. He never wanted to let her go! He couldn't risk losing her again! But then he saw the florist box out of the corner of his eye. "Oh, I almost forgot! These are for you." He opened the box and she saw the roses.

"Do you remember saying Mr. Right would bring you roses?" She laughed, nodded, and wiped the tears from her eyes. Daryl suddenly knew, he finally found his angel because God sent a letter with gold wings and silver letters, NAJ, and Daryl Baker's faith was rewarded.

Chapter 8 ~ *Pastor Hugh Hayden's Story*

Edward Hayden and Martha Emerson married in 1960 on Christmas Eve. They dreamed of a house full of little Haydens to fill their home with laughter and memories.

On June 30th, 1965, they became the proud parents of a son, Hubert Emerson Hayden; the name he preferred was Hugh. Only by the grace of God did Martha conceive. Edward and Martha fasted after Pastor O'Steen preached about Hannah from the Old Testament. She was also barren til God moved.

Edward was a strong man of God and Martha was from a strong Christian family as well. So their faith was great and in October of 1964, Martha conceived and the baby was born the following June. He was dedicated to the Lord immediately and the family was blessed.

They taught their son the laws and ordinances of God according to scripture. The Bible was the deciding manual in every choice they made. *Nothing* was accepted that crossed that line. The Hayden family attended church as if services were their umbilical cords, that connected them to the heart of God. And there was nothing that could keep them out of the God's house!

In 1972, Rebecca was born when Martha went into labor *at* church; devotion was woven into their culture. But no one ever felt the need to explain to the lanky, spectacled fourteen year old lad that there was a deeper, spiritual 'choice' made by his parents and his grandparents. So God spoke to him through an anointed message that changed the world around him.

One Sunday afternoon, Hugh calmly said, "Dad, I won't be going to the evening service tonight. My band director called us together and told us we need to go over the music we're performing at the band

-118-

competition next week. We will all meet in the gymnasium but he said he'll see that I get home safely after the practice."

Edward Hayden set his coffee cup back on the table, and carefully said, "When you speak to your band director, you tell him I appreciate his offer to see you home safely. But it won't be necessary, Hugh."

He hurriedly tried to explain to his father. "But he said he'll be driving most of the guys home, so it really won't be a problem for him..."

He left out the part where the group would be stopping for pizza after the practice. He knew his dad would *not* approve of missing church to attend a pizza party. It wasn't dishonest, Hugh reasoned in his own mind, since the main reason he would be missing was for band competition practice; the pizza was just ... a reward.

But Edward Hayden raised his hand and said, "No, son, I'm telling you it won't be *necessary* because you won't *be* there tonight. Sundays are the days we give ourselves to God to rest in Him. The band director will just have to make due with one of the other six days, and you *will* give him your best work when he does."

Hugh started to object, but he knew there was nothing else to be said that would change his father's mind. His expression said it all. That night, a somber teenager sat next to his parents at church. He wondered how he would explain his absence to the band director and the others at his school. He would probably be laughed at. Hugh's face reddened at the thought.

He glanced quickly to see if anyone noticed his embarrassment but everyone had closed their eyes in prayer. Hugh breathed a sigh of relief. 'Thank You, God,' he mumbled. And the preacher said, "Amen."

Then his eyes seemed to be fixed on Hugh. He spoke directly to him as if no one else was there! (Hugh was sure of it). "When I was a child, I spake as a child, I understood as a child, I thought as a child; but when I became a man, I put away all my childish things."

Hugh swallowed hard, staring into the face of Reverend O'Steen. This was serious! He wasn't sure why, but he could feel both palms of his hands getting clammy. Why was *he* the one the preacher singled out? Did the whole congregation know the pastor was only speaking to him?

Just then, the minister turned and expounded on his message, "When you are a child, everything is new yet defined by our boundaries. Our parents, and our schools, and our friends, all are boundary 'makers,' who *we* follow like sheep. The question is, *where*, my friend? Where will you *go* with these boundary 'makers'? How far and in what direction? It *had better* be to the Lord! *He* will *not* abandon you, NO!"

The pastor shook his head to sternly emphasize how strong God's love is for His children. Then his voice changed, becoming soft and gentle as he spoke to them, "You're His *precious child*, the Apple of His eye! He has a plan for you, called Salvation and it's all in this one Instruction Book, the Bible, the unerring, infallible Word of the Living God!"

Then the tone of his voice lowered to nearly a whisper, "Or ... you may choose ... to refuse ... God..." Suddenly, the man of God became very quiet, laying his Bible on the altar. "I could tell you about a place of agony and eternal hell." He shook his head sadly.

The minister walked back to the Hayden family who sat together on the third row. He laid his hand on the boy's head. He closed his eyes and lifted his face towards heaven.

He said, "But just like the cycle in life, a baby is born and a seed is within him to choose a path his life will follow. There will be times of doubts... fears and choices. But it is *our* responsibility to supply that child with the necessary wisdom to make good, spiritual choices.

Pastor O'Steen turned to face the congregation, "*Choose* to spend eternity with Jesus Christ! *Choose* life and *cast aside* the deceiver who can only offer you suffering and eternal hell."

Hugh looked at his parents who were smiling and nodding. Edward Hayden had tears in his closed eyes, praying and exalting God for His wonderful plan of salvation.

That night, Hugh stood to his feet, knees knocking and hands shaking. He walked up to the front of the altar. His voice was cracking when he proclaimed to his pastor, "I choose God, Pastor!"

Reverend O'Steen led him in the sinner's prayer and the young man knew he would devote his life to leading wayward souls to God.

The Hayden house was full of celebration that evening. A big dinner was prepared and a cake was baked in honor of Hugh's life changing decision. Even Rebecca, his younger sister, was excited about her creative flair, frosting the cake and writing, "Happy Birthday, again!"

The 'born again' experience was not taken lightly by the Hayden family. Edward Hayden gave a little talk about the honor of giving birth, bringing the gift of a new life into the world, and all the important obligations that followed in the natural world.

He said the gift of salvation, the 'born again' experience, was not to be entered into lightly. It was to begin life anew in the Spirit and our responsibility was to honor the Savior for His sacrifice on the cross.

The mandatory commitments to the kingdom of God, were never to be casual, but must be life changing covenants with our Omnipotent God."

Hugh looked around the room and vowed that he would never forget any of those faces that smiled back at him, loving, encouraging him. Edward sat at the head of the table, full of pride for his young son. His mother brought food to the table and Rebecca filled the water glasses.

Next week he would be baptized at the river. All things at the Haydens were governed by spiritual rites of passage.

Soon Rebecca would be celebrating her salvation.

God was in control and His will would unequivocally be done in the home of Edward Hayden. Anyone who ever visited the Haydens expected their home to be an open haven and a storehouse of love.

There was once an immigrant man, by the name of Jackson who settled outside of Forest Hills with his family. He lived in a humble cottage at the foothills of the mountains. Mr. Jackson, a quiet man, had a gentle and friendly nature. He respected Hugh's father, Edward, but the Jacksons did not attend the Forest Hills Church of Faith. In fact, no one knew very much about their beliefs or customs.

He was a 'jack-of-all-trades,' and he was always the first to volunteer his expertise and labor whenever and wherever he was needed. But one year, he helped a neighbor install solar panels and stayed on the job later than usual. He walked the usual path towards their cottage, noticing the sunset but the horizon had an eerie glow.

As he neared his home, he could smell burning embers. In agony he watched his cottage fall to the ground, leaving nothing behind but the stench of death. Jenny, his wife, and his little daughter, Marisol, perished in the fire. The grief-strickened man dropped to his knees and wept.

The fire marshall notified Edward Hayden and he came quickly to Mr. Jackson's side. But the man was despondent, apparently in shock and barely could answer the fire marshall's questions.

Edward put his arm around the man's shoulder and said, "Come my friend, let's go home. Martha has dinner waiting. You will stay with me as long as you need us." Then he led the old man away like a little boy and took him home to be nurtured and restored. There he could find peace.

He stayed with the family, observing Edward's strong Christian foundation and soon he desired all the strength he witnessed in him.

Edward Hayden prayed daily for his guest, that he could share the love of God with him. Yet after two weeks, the guest was still quiet, showing no outward desire for God.

Edward quietly fasted his evening meal, and he prayed fervently by his bedside that God would soon restore his guest. Then, one evening, the man asked him, "Edward, what is it you do each night at mealtime? I see you push back your plate following grace and you go to your room. Who is it you are speaking with? And you must tell me why do you cry out the way you do?"

That night, Hugh saw a light in his father's eyes as he led the man aside. He said, "Mr. Jackson, this will be a day you will never forget, for *this day* you will have a new heart. God *will* speak to you in your spirit and give you purpose. You will become a man of God, a new spirit.

I will teach you of a man I call Jesus who said, 'The Spirit of the Lord is upon me to preach the gospel to the poor; He has sent me to heal the brokenhearted, to proclaim liberty to the captives and recovery of sight to the blind; To set at liberty those who are oppressed; to proclaim the acceptable year of the Lord. And we are to follow in the footsteps of Jesus."

That night the guest was saved and the next morning, he was gone and they never heard from him again. But others came and said the home was a lighthouse in their storm. That was the foundation Hugh Hayden was saved on. Twenty-two years ago...

Twenty-two years ago! Was it that long ago? Hugh Hayden paused and reflected on those years. And it all started the night when he wished the doors of the church were closed for a Sunday evening service. He thanked God his father was wise enough to stand on his covenant with God.

He wished the board at Forest Hills was just as strong. At each board meeting, the subject of evening services was voted on. But Hugh was determined to keep the doors open as long as he was the pastor! Where would he be today if his church had not been open on that Sunday night, twenty-two years ago?

-123-

Hugh glanced up and noticed Deacon Kirby motioning to him. He was holding an envelope and needed to speak to him. Hugh appreciated his friend Deacon Kirby. He and his wife supported the pastor a hundred percent, and also encouraged him through prayer. He loved him like a brother! And Sister Kirby was a real prayer warrior! Without a doubt, they were sent by God.

Hugh asked, "Did you need to see me, brother?" The pastor unlocked his office door inviting the elder to enter. Deacon Kirby said, "This envelope was given to me at Katie Pearson's funeral. He said it was very important that you receive it today! I have no idea who sent it but *you* need to check it out."

Hugh held the envelope and knew immediately it was from NAJ. The envelope was very familiar; the golden wings were a giveaway. 'Oh, who could be the next recipient of the elusive gift benefactor?'

He added, "Oh, and there's a message on your desk, too. Someone was here earlier today, Michael somebody. Anyways, he left his card. I think he's a lawyer. He says he's trying to locate a man named Neimann Jackson, whoever he is. I told him I knew he wasn't a member of our congregation here but he left his card in case we can help in any way."

Hugh laughed, "Is there anything in that note on my desk you haven't already told me?" Hugh smiled as his friend answered quickly, "I'm just watchin' your back, Preacher. That's what I'm here for!"

Hugh patted his back and grinned, "I know you are, brother, and I appreciate it." He opened the letter and read the message inside. In beautiful script was written, *"Luke Chapter 2 tells us the angel said, "Behold, I bring you tidings of great joy." The Savior was being born! Today we are still singing His praises!" Please join the Hospice Center on Christmas Eve at 7 pm. for caroling and fellowship. Please bring along your musicians and singers for God is truly worthy to be praised!"*

What a lovely invitation! And what a surprise! Hugh smiled and he thought how excited the choir would be to share their Christmas cantata with the patients.

Sunday evening the choir was scheduled to begin practicing so he wrote a memo to remind himself to announce the event during the practice. Then he returned the letter to it's angel-winged envelope and thanked God for it.

The sopranos took their positions in the choir loft and the altos stood to the right. The baritones and a precious eighty-nine year old man, Eugene Grubbs, who sang bass, stood talking by the altars. Hugh stood in the foyer and watched the twelve members of the choir. He was proud of their talents and willingness to use their voices for God.

"Good evening! I hope everybody is in good voice because we have just received a beautiful invitation to sing our Christmas carols for the Hospice Center on Christmas Eve!"

The choir members were thrilled as they started planning which songs would be the favorites for their audience! "We need to get busy! We only have a few practice sessions before we sing for them!"

Hugh laughed. It brought him great pleasure to hear the excitement in these good people at Christmas! No murmuring or complaints were heard, just joy! At the end of the practice session, Hugh reminded them to meet at the church at six p.m. on Christmas Eve and they would all travel together in the church bus.

Eugene Grubbs said in his slow quiet voice, "I think we ought to put down all the windows so we can sing all the way to the center! And that way our songs would be heard by most of the townsfolk, too."

He added, "But you better dress warm, 'cause we're supposed to have a white Christmas!" The rest of the choir members laughed but they all agreed that he had a good idea. Christmas carols would fill the night air in Forest Hills on Christmas Eve!

A light snow had fallen; glistening trees sparkled

in the moonlight. The brightly colored Christmas lights reflected against the snowkissed lawns. Candles glowed in the windows; a life sized nativity scene was placed in the town square. Currier and Ives could not have painted more tranquility. Just one word could describe the beauty on the earth's canvas of Forest Hills... Christmas!

The nurses greeted the carolers who came inside singing, 'We wish you a Merry Christmas, we wish you a Merry Christmas!'

The ambulatory patients came out to the atrium, in brightly colored robes and slippers. Those confined by tubes and monitors were visited by the strolling minstrels; tears of gratitude filled their eyes. What a wonderful holiday custom, bringing Christmas joy to the shut-ins!

Bethany Pearson was the R.N. on duty and she was bubbling over with news that her son, Jacob invited his scout troop to their home in Rose Court. While they were there, they decided to help decorate for Christmas. She told the staff she had very few ornaments and lights but when 'Ben,' the new scout-master arrived, he created a real winter wonderland for her. They found mistletoe, too, but as Bethany quickly added, "It's too soon for that!"

But it looks like the young, single, scoutmaster could be interested in building a snowman named 'Parson Brown' in the meadow, with a certain nurse. Bethany glowed with her new found happiness!

There were six seats placed at each round table in the dining hall. Each table had a red, green, or gold tablecloth with a candle centerpiece. The carolers complimented the staff on the holiday décor.

There were small groups moving through the halls and corridors, bringing Christmas cheer, friends greeting friends. Hugh smiled and shook hands with the staff, turning around to see the musicians setting up their instruments.

"Wasn't this an excellent idea to share Christmas with hospice?" Hugh commented to a group nearby.

Michael Genucci, an attorney with Omega Investments, Ltd. (and an unexpected guest), replied, "Yes! This is a wonderful gathering! I've not seen such enthusiasm since I left the old country!"

Hugh turned to see the face of the man who left his business card at the church office. Now Pastor Hayden sensed the man's urgency to find closure to his quest.

The minister offered an outstretched hand, "You must be Michael Genucci. I've seen your card and I heard you have come to Forest Hills hoping to find a missing person?"

He paused and felt his Spirit quicken. What was this man's real reason for coming to Forest Hills and why did Hugh's spirit react so strongly? So he waited.

"I'm sorry, sir, I must apologize to you. Please forgive me for being so intrusive on your festivities. But I feel as though I know all of you.

I have been in your beautiful country for quite some time now. I have been searching for a man, who I am starting to believe, has never existed at all! His name is Neimann Jackson and he was born in Malta. Please tell me on this holiest of nights, that you have at least heard of him. It would at least give me hope that I have not searched for him in vain."

"Sir, I'm sorry. I wish I had something to tell you. I've been pastoring in Forest Hills for the past several years and I don't believe I've ever heard of Neimann Jackson..."

"Did somebody call my name?" An elderly man opened a door and then pulled it closed behind him. "I am Neimann Jackson." Mr. Genucci, was full of questions. His response was one of surprise, "*You* are Neimann Jackson? Did I not meet with you months ago? I believed then that you convinced me you were *not* the man for whom I was searching. Sir, do you remember when we last spoke?"

Neimann laughed, "Of course, I do! What do you think? That I'm an old man?" Hugh chuckled. 'This 'old man' sure was a quick thinker!' The lawyer

-127-

cleared his throat and humbly apologized, "No, sir, I did not mean to imply that you were..." The old man waved his hand. "It's okay, son, I'm just teasing you."

Michael said, "I asked you before if you were the same Neimann Jackson who came from Malta in 1956 and you said, 'No, I am not.' Was that not your response?" The old man smiled and said, "Well, some questions can often have more than one answer. Did I leave Malta in 1956? Yes, I did. Am I the same man? No, I am not."

Michael looked at Manny and smiled. "You are as I have been told, an amazing character! Could we go somewhere private so we can speak of Malta and our mutual acquaintances?"

Manny nodded and gently leaned on Michael's arm for support as he slowly walked with him down the hallway of the Hospice Health Center. An open door beckoned them to enter and share their precious moments and closed as if an angel stood watch over them.

Chapter 9 ~ *Manny's Story*

The time had come for Manny to meet Michael. The young attorney looked at Manny and asked him, "Have you been avoiding me?" Manny said, "No, son, just completing the work I have been called to do."

Michael studied the old man's face and asked, "Do you know who I am?" Manny smiled, "Michael, my Father prepares me for many events, so I *do* know the reason for your visit to me at this time. But I am not sure that *you* fully understand the reason *you* have been sent to find *me*."

Michael opened his brief case and handed him a letter of introduction. With tearful eyes, Manny read the words of the dying man he had come to respect like a father.

He sent his love to Manny, saying, "My dear son, Neimann: Many years have past since we have last spoken. But I am certain you are well and happy in your new land.

I have watched you with great pleasure while I followed your successful life. You have richly blessed me with your deep compassion for the families of God. It is for this cause I write to you now.

Man has little time to share his life before he is called to venture into eternity. As you have learned, eternal destination is determined by the choices and pathways chosen in life. I don't need to tell you that. For you have grasped that concept and built your life upon it. But now my Lord has led me to find an heir to the vast fortune God has bestowed upon me.

This is why I have selected my young grandson, Michael Genucci, to be the heir and executor of my estate. But this is cannot be granted until I am sure that he has attained the spiritual wisdom and insight you have demonstrated in your life. This legacy cannot be taken lightly.

For that reason, I have sent Michael to find you through his own devices and to learn your ways. Once this has been accomplished, such a gift as the one I presented to you so many years ago in Malta, will also be passed on to Michael. Your crown is mighty, Neimann! The jewels you have earned in your crown of righteousness are unsurpassed.

You have proven your wisdom gained on your journey as I observed your ways. Each gift you were able to present to God's chosen ones, was given with much planning and forethought. The lessons they were taught through the administering of God's Word will never be forgotten nor taken lightly.

That is my desire for Michael. His quest to serve God must be as diligent and as solemn as the years you have spent on your mission to seek the will of God.

You chose wisely when you sought your spiritual counsel from Edward Hayden and I pray that Michael will also find a man of God such as this to guide him in his future. I anxiously wait to greet you soon, my son, at our Father's table. Signed, Antonio De Sensa."

The old man smiled as he wiped his eyes. He said, "Mr. Tony. How I loved him!" He sighed and said, "Now, Michael, I must tell you about a very special journey. You will hear of miracles and untold mysteries. You will learn incredible skills but first you must learn to listen, not as a man but as a spirit in tune with God."

Manny began to speak and he listened to the old man's amazing life. "It all *started* in Malta. The year was 1919. I was born in a tiny fishing village but my parents died when I was an infant.

My Aunt Berta raised me and taught me to be honest and to work hard. She said, 'Neimann, it is a gift from God to sweat and labor long and hard!' So each day she told me to look after my neighbors. If I could help them in any way, it was my duty!

But there were times I could go to the docks and watch as the fishermen hauled in the catch. It was amazing! My friend, Oscar, who was about a year older than I, would make up wonderful tales about a future as two world famous fishermen!" Then Manny paused, reflecting on his memories.

"We rolled up the cuffs of our pant legs and wore matching fishing hats. Your grandfather, (we all called him Mr. Tony), gave us our first fishing caps. He told us if we wore them every day, we would be sure to catch lots of fish! We all loved Mr. Tony. I saw him quite often when I did chores for the older people in the village. Oscar and I were together all the time except when I had to work. Oscar told me we were going to be two champion fishermen and sail around the world!"

Michael smiled, as he imagined the dreams of the children. "Our final destination would be the United States of America. We had plans to buy a mountain and start our own country there!" Manny laughed, "Oscar was such a dreamer, but he wasn't so good with his geography though." Manny laughed.

"He said we would build big mansions someday for us to live in. And every day we would start the morning by fishing in *both* mighty oceans and in the evenings, we would rest by the giant waterfalls. The skies would be full of stars that would shine on our bright new kingdom! Poor Oscar." Manny shook his head and smiled.

Michael asked, "So then, his big dreams never happened?" Manny took a sip of water and nodded, "In a way. When he was thirteen he came to America. His family bought a piece of real estate on Backbone Mountain, so they *did* live on a mountain there. But there were no oceans or giant waterfalls for him."

Michael said, "I was on Backbone Mountain not long ago when I was searching for you. How did *you* get to America?" Manny closed his eyes, remembering the past.

"Oscar wrote to me often. He met a wonderful lady named Matilda and they fell in love. Soon they were married and had a son, Daryl. But it wasn't my time to come yet. There were many friends in Malta who depended on me. When I graduated from high school, the whole village had a party for me. I was very surprised!" Manny's eyes were wide as he told the story to Michael.

"There were all kinds of food and music! Mr. Tony showed up and made a speech about the great things I would accomplish in my lifetime.

My heart was full but I had no idea how I could ever accomplish such great things in the fishing village where I lived. But the people cheered loudly! Aunt Berta was so proud!"

Manny looked down and said in a solemn voice, "Then I got ... *the gift.* It changed my life! It was an envelope, a very special envelope, soft and tinted. In the upper left corner was a heart with the letters, AD. I remember gently touching the envelope and asking Mr. Tony, 'What is this?'

He told me he loved me like a son. He pointed to the heart and said, 'See this? I send you with my love, my heart. I asked him what AD stood for. He said, 'It is just a reminder that Antonio De Sensa... A.D... sends you with his heart. Open it, son.'"

Manny's voice cracked as he said, "He gave me a life! It was a paid scholarship to the University de Milan in Italy. He gave me a chance of a lifetime, an extensive education in engineering! Then he sent me with a letter of introduction to his friend, a professor who studied the properties of Polymer Science.

I worked there for five years, studying under the tutelage of gifted men of science, brilliant men who would go on to win the Nobel Prize! I was soon associated with them so I was sent to many countries on five great continents! I sat in conferences with men of power, influential men, heads of state! I was affiliated with charitable organizations; we set up foundations to help veterans and handicapped of all ages plus little homeless children.

Soon I was sought after night and day. I knew I had fortune and fame. But it wasn't enough. I would have traded it all for the quiet life my friend, Oscar had found with his lovely wife, Matilda in America."

Manny stood and walked to the window where he could see the pastor shaking hands with the other patients. He stood there with his hands clasped behind his back and smiled.

"But then I met a beautiful lady named Jenny. She was my best friend. When I asked her to marry me, she said, 'Yes!' But I don't think she knew what her life was going to be like.

The media heard of our wedding abd soon it was like a circus! We were bombarded with reporters and cameras. We hardly knew those at our own wedding!"

He smiled mischievously, "So I gave her the best wedding gift in the world! At midnight, we flew to Backbone Mountain in America. I landed our plane just a few miles from Oscar's home in Eagle's Nest Estates. Oscar was delighted and two old friends were reunited as though we had never been apart! Oscar and Matilda kept my secret as long as they lived!

We lived a very reclusive life, in a little cottage close to the railroad tracks south of Backbone Mountain. It was private and had a little lake on the property. Jenny and I were very happy there... until she died." Manny's voice broke with emotion.

He cleared his throat as he spoke about his wife and child. The memory was still very painful for him. "We had a baby girl and we named her Marisol. She was so beautiful! The image of her Mama!"

Michael said, "Where is your daughter now, sir?" Manny cleared his throat again as he told him, "She ...died in the fire... with Jenny. My Marisol was just nine years old. She was still my baby girl."

Michael was sorry he asked; he shook his head as Manny continued. "I wasn't home. I was busy back then. If a neighbor began a project, Manny was there to lend a hand. After all, they were neighbors.

I never told anyone where I learned to be a good builder, electrician, or a plumber... I think they called me a 'Jack of all trades.' No one knew I held many degrees and many prestigious positions. Everyone just assumed I was a poor immigrant who Oscar took in.

It suited my need for a private life.

But with all my experience and education, I have learned the most important lessons from love." Michael asked, "Is that what Grandfather wants me to learn from you? To value life with family and friends over material gain?" Manny nodded slowly, "That's only a part of it.

Michael, when Jenny and Marisol died in that fire, I lost the will to live. I couldn't understand why man was put on earth to suffer the grief I felt in my heart. I had many experiences in life but not one gave me a purpose or a reason to want to go on living!"

Michael listened closely. "You must have found a way to cope. You seem to be contented with your life now." Manny paused as Michael slowly phrased his next question: "What has made the difference in your life?" Manny smiled and patted the younger man's hand. "Not what... Who, Michael... "

Michael leaned back in his chair waiting for an explanation. Manny hesitated as he searched for just the right words. "After the fire, a man of God came to me. I was devastated. The undertaker came and he took my family away and I realized I was alone. My friend, Oscar had died almost seven years before and I was curious as to why I was left behind to live."

Michael nodded, "I understand why you would feel that way." Manny continued, "Edward Hayden was a neighbor, very highly respected in our little community. He never hesitated. He came to get me and said, "Mr. Jackson, let's go home. Martha has dinner ready."

It was as if we had been brothers for life and we were really going home to our family! He made me a part of his life that quickly! He was an amazing man! He was... a *Friend* of *God*!"

Michael watched Manny's eyes light up. "Why was this man so special, Mr. Jackson? Because he helped you deal with your loss? What was different about him? Why do you say he was a *Friend* of God?"

Manny paused, "He never once asked for a thing from me. He just shared his life, his family and his faith. His love and his compassion was like the love of God... unconditional! My pain became his sadness. My grief was a prison of darkness. But then, he gave me Jesus to light my way."

Manny was weighing his words carefully. "He was able to show me how to become a new person through God! Once I was lost but I have now been found, I'm saved, and I'm adopted into the Kingdom of God. I am no longer the same Neimann Jackson who came from Malta. I can barely remember him. "

Michael was confused. "Then, who is this new, *elusive* Neimann Jackson you say you've become? The old man smiled and said, "God has ordained my life and given me many blessings. But blessings are meant to be shared, not hoarded." Manny closed his eyes.

"For many years I have been able to fund big foundations and it has made me famous. How much more should I do for God for His people? He must surely deserve much more than I. His people, all the children of God, need a blessing now and then. And so He sends me when He needs me. It is not Neimann who can be praised, but the hand of God and His mercy."

Michael searched Manny's eyes desperate for a clue to the understanding he needed. If only he could interpret the depths of wisdom and experience within the man's heart. This was Michael's heartfelt prayer! Then as if a window opened, he had a moment of fresh awakening... an anointing! The key to the life of Neimann Aaron Jackson was gifted to him! Suddenly he understood the life calling of Neimann Jackson!

After Edward Hayden led him to the Lord, he set out on a quest few men have ever ventured. He *literally* searched the Word of God for a purpose for his life. As he drew closer to God, he developed an amazing relationship with Him. The Omnipotent, Lord of Lords and King of Kings... was his Father!

Manny developed excellence in his integrity and

achievements. He refused to give less to God. Michael looked away, remembering the morning prayer spoken by his Grandfather Antonio, "Father let Your children see... the Hand of God... at work in Me."

Manny said softly, "It feels strange to speak of this. I have remained anonymous for many years. Your grandfather was the only one I confided in. He sent a supply of Crane envelopes, the finest stationery in the world!" Manny handed him a sample of the paper.

"Your grandfather had them all embossed with gold angel wings for he felt that I was a messenger of God, like angels with wings in the scriptures. He made them gold for the precious golden streets inside heaven. Then he created a symbol of my three initials in silver to be held lovingly in the wings, for that was his prayer for me... to be safe and loved."

Michael was very impressed as he touched the soft texture on Manny's stationery. "But I don't fully understand, sir. Why did you use these envelopes? With whom did you correspond?"

Manny laughed, "With whomever He sent me to. I have become quite familiar with my Father's voice. He leads my steps. Sometimes I am called to provide someone shelter, or transportation. Sometimes it may be a ticket to a land far away. There are times for a trust fund to be set up. But whatever the deed is, it is *always* done for the good of God's people and for His glory!

The envelopes are simply a means to notify the recipient of the blessing. The symbolic angel's wings show God's compassion, embracing us like my insignia, NAJ, serving as a reminder that our Lord, Jehovah-Jireh, will always be our Provider."

Michael lowered his head and said softly, "What must I do to have the mantle you wear in this life?" Manny placed his hands on Michael's shoulders and said, "When a man is willing to place his life and all he treasures in the hands of God, miracles happen, prayers are answered, lives are altered and the angels go to work!

For the *body* of Christ, or the *believers* of Christ, are indeed *bodies* for Christ. What we see, hear, and speak must be in a direct correlation with the will of the Father in heaven. But first you must accept Jesus in your heart." Michael nodded, saying, "I do need Jesus to fill my heart." Tears filled Manny's eyes as he began to lead Michael in the sinner's prayer. The room was filled with the presence of the Holy Spirit, as the holy mantle was passed down once more.

Pastor Hugh Hayden watched as the two men entered Manny's room down the hall. Manny's room, 17, was cozy. Each brightly painted room had twin beds with striped ivory, rose, or gold Riviera quilts. There were matching curtains hung at the two small jalousied windows, slightly cranked open to allow a breeze to enter the room during the holiday festivities. They closed the door quietly behind them.

It was wonderful to see them together. They had obviously shared many stories of Malta, about families and mutual friends. Manny's step seemed to be much lighter now. His shoulders had been stooped and his spine showed years of hard work and aging. But now there seemed to be something vaguely familiar about him.

Hugh watched Michael leave Manny's room. He probably wanted to let him rest. The young attorney glowed, smiling at Hugh. "I wish I had known your father. He must have been an incredible man."

Hugh stopped and said, "My father? Yes, he was a great man... but..." Michael said, "Mr. Jackson was just telling me how your family took him in after the fire claimed the lives of Jenny and Marisol.

Hugh felt his jaw drop in disbelief. 'That was Mr. Jackson?!' He paused and said, "Neimann... Aaron... Jackson! N... A... J!" He turned and said, "That's unbelievable! But he was an old man when I was just..." Hugh's voice trailed off, "Is it possible?"

He quickly turned, to look towards Room 17. Michael laughed. "Yes, sir. With God, *all* things are possible. I just learned that tonight." He explained to

Hugh how the man's life brought him to Forest Hills and his mission that Michael must now pursue. He concluded with, "I think he truly deserves the rest he's enjoying tonight."

Hugh agreed and said, "But I just have to look in on him now that I know who he is. I'll try not to disturb him if he's asleep."

He tapped lightly on the door but heard nothing. The door creaked slightly, so he entered slowly. The windows left open brought cool air into the room, the curtains fluttered in the wind. Outside, a light snowfall had settled on the lawn and the moon glowed brightly upon Room 17.

A beautiful scent lingered unlike any fragrance he had ever known. But something was missing in here. Neimann Aaron Jackson was gone! But how? There were no other exits! The windows were not large enough for even a child to pass through! Mr. Jackson just simply... vanished!

Hugh softly quoted Genesis 5:24, "And Enoch walked with God: and he was not; for God took him." A note, left on the table, addressed to Michael read, "I'll be waiting for you at the Father's table."

Signed, Neimann Aaron Jackson, NAJ.

Chapter 10 ~ *Afterwords*

The residents of Forest Hills were gathering all over town to talk about the disappearance of the old man. The explanations varied from 'he wandered off and the center didn't want to get bad publicity...' to 'aliens must have captured him.' Of course, those who had the amazing opportunity of meeting the man... or received an 'odd letter' had no doubt he was an angel or at least a special soul who was carried to heaven. One thing everyone agreed on... he would be missed.

Pastor Hugh Hayden arranged for a memorial service to be held at the Forest Hills Church of Faith on New Year's Eve. They always had a watchnight service but this year the service would be different. This would be a year to give thanks to God for sending Manny to Forest Hills and the chance to learn from the incredible man of God.

But there were those who needed to be comforted before the memorial and a lot of loose ends had to be handled.

The first to telephone the church office was the director of Hospice, Martin Burdine. "Good morning, Pastor Hayden, this is Martin Burdine with the local Hospice Center."

Hugh knew Martin from the Businessmen's Association. Most of the churches in the area belonged to the group as well as the Chamber of Commerce. The director was a well-educated man, a retired physician, and past president of the Chamber. But one thing he was not, was a Christian. He was having a hard time accepting the explanation that one of his patients had simply disappeared. But even more on his mind, were the legal ramifications.

"Reverend, do you know if Neimann Jackson had any next of kin to notify? More specifically, sir, are there any relatives who may attempt legal action?"

The pastor wearily shook his head, "Martin, I

don't think you have a thing to worry about. But if you're interested, our church will be having Mr. Jackson's memorial service on New Year's Eve as a kind of tribute during our watchnight service. We plan to meet at the church at ten p.m. on December 31st. You are welcome to come and anyone from Hospice as well."

The director cleared his throat and said, "Well, I don't think we'll will be able to come to your service, Pastor Hayden. We try to steer clear of any denominational affiliation so we don't offend anyone at hospice. But, sir, if you happen to notice anyone at his memorial who may be related or have any legal connection, you will let me know, won't you?"

Hugh didn't think Mr. Burdine would come. He would never deny the patients their right to worship in any church they chose, but he was quick to admit to being an atheist. But Hugh invited him just in case. After all, miracles were in season! "Yes, of course, sir, if I have any news, I'll be sure to let you know. And if you hear any news, I'll expect the same courtesy. Good day, Mr. Burdine."

By ten o'clock on Monday morning,, seven people had called to ask for details on the memorial service planned for Manny. It was going to be one of the most unusual events Hugh ever organized. There was no deceased, no pictures and no family that anyone knew about. But just to be sure, he decided to put a small announcement in the local newspaper.

On New Year's Eve, Hugh opened the church at eight p.m. and a couple of cars followed him into the parking lot. He recognized Edie Henson's car and the new Hyundai that Bethany purchased last year.

When he saw the 1985 Lincoln Town Car, though, something stirred in his spirit. Hugh saw the Lincoln around town several times. He always stopped to look at the vehicle. Someone obviously loved that car; it was immaculate! But he never met the owner. He was surprised when he saw Daryl open the driver's door and step out.

Nicole, with her two little girls, Thien and Tuyen, followed Daryl into the parking lot driving her white Elantra. Hugh had been counselling Daryl and Nicole for a couple of weeks. They wanted to be married on Valentine's Day. The two precious daughters were both going be flower girls in the wedding.

Deacon and Sister Kirby were parking their car next to the office entrance. Tommie, another board member opened the office door for them and, seeing the pastor, hurried to speak to him.

"Pastor, have you been inside the church yet?" Brother Tommie was troubled. "I know we ordered a centerpiece of flowers from the florist, but that's not what we got. I know what was ordered, brother. I was the one who wrote it down and I heard the secretary make the call. We called the florist next to the Pleasant Grove Hospital. The lady told us she would take care of everything. But brother Hugh, you are not going to believe this!"

The pastor tried to understand the problem as he walked into the church with Brother Tommie. He was one of the newest deacons and he took his job very seriously. With Brother Tommie, there was always a reason and a receipt for every purchase. But obviously the order for the flowers was not filled as planned.

"Brother, if a mistake was made, I'm sure a call to the florist will take care of it. Relax, okay?" But the deacon shook his head, "Pastor, I don't think you are aware just how *big* a mistake was made!"

As the church doors opened, the foyer was overflowing with flowers! An archway of lilies topped the french doors. Carnations and roses sprayed across the altar and oriental liles and floral arrangements filled the sanctuary. In the choir loft, a fountain was placed flanked with white columns, rocks and floating lilies. "I know we didn't order all this, Pastor. Our budget won't afford all this!"

Brother Tommie was determined to resolve this issue... somehow! Hugh opened the door to his office to call the owner of the business at home... no one would be in the office but he knew the owner, Estelle Owens. She would quickly settle the mixup.

Estelle moved to Forest Hills three years ago. She had been married several years to Clarence Owens, a truck driver who traveled a lot. His job involved long hours of driving and long distance hauling. Like so many of the men and women in his profession, he began to depend on drugs to keep awake...and to go to sleep... and soon the drugs *were* his life.

After being battered by her husband, (whose drug addiction consumed him), Estelle left Clarence and her home in Pennsylvania and moved to Forest Hills. She had no family or friends here but soon she opened the florist shop across the street from the hospital. She was active in the Nazarene Church and a member of the choir.

First ring... second... third... answering machine. Estelle was not available. But Hugh was confident she would handle the problem. "Brother Tommie, we can't reach the florist right now, so what do you think? I say we give it to God and get on with the memorial. How about it?" The deacon shrugged, "It's your call, Pastor. I just wanted you to know, we didn't order all these flowers."

As the men left the office, they saw Estelle enter the church. "So what do you think, Brother Hayden, aren't they lovely? My girls sure do good work, don't they?"

"Estelle, I never expected to see you here! We ordered the flowers to honor Neimann Jackson, but we only expected a nice floral arrangement! I'm glad to see you, but I am surprised that you came!"

"Hugh, the notice you ran in the paper said the memorial was to honor Neimann Jackson but when I read that 'NAJ' was the honoree, I knew I had to be here.

'NAJ' set me up in my florist business when I had no one to turn to. I never knew who he was. I received an odd letter which held the deed to the shop and my first shipment of stock was completely paid for in advance so all I needed was customers. Oh, and by the way, all the flowers are on me. It's the least I can do."

"You received a letter from 'NAJ'?" Hugh began to wonder how far his generosity reached in Forest Hills... or beyond? He was wondering how to start the memorial service and God sent Estelle to guide him. She would be the first to speak of Manny's Gift... his love for Jehovah-Jireh and his mission to share God's love for His children.

Hugh stood before a congregation that filled every seat in the sanctuary... and still they kept coming! The men began placing folding chairs in the aisles and the crowds began to stand outside the doors of the Forest Hills Church of Faith as they came to honor Neimann Jackson, NAJ.

The pastor welcomed the community, telling them about an amazing man who became a friend of God. "Manny preferred to remain anonymous, that God's hand would be all that could be seen. But Neimann Jackson was a man of integrity and compassion. He set out on his life's mission to follow the footsteps of Jesus, who went about doing good!" And now I would like to introduce the woman who so graciously donated these beautiful flowers."

Brother Tommie smiled and shook his head. 'God has done it again,' he thought. 'He took a stumbling block, a crisis, and turned it into a stepping stone to resolve a problem.'

Estelle explained how she was spiritually depleted after years of abuse. She was lacking confidence and had no collateral or credit to start up a business. Her most fulfilling memories were the summers she spent with her grandmother who had several greenhouses. The old woman loved plants and Estelle grew up with experience and a love for gardening.

Clarence never shared her passion for growing her plants and landscaping. (In his mind they were all weeds). She soon laid aside her dreams and believed she was destined to follow his... to own his own rig. It was a dream he pursued vigorously and each time his plan collapsed, he blamed Estelle.

Soon he started striking out at her verbally in his frustration. But then came the bruises, and fractures. When her divorce was granted, the only thing she had to show for all her years of marriage were crutches and X-rays.

When she came to Forest Hills a letter arrived. It had gold wings and silver letters in the return address corner. The letter told her to read Matthew 6: 25-34. The scriptures encouraged her to seek God first and not worry about how she would survive alone. God would provide. But verses 28 and 29 got her heart racing! The 28th verse said, "Consider the Lilies of the field..." and the 29th verse said, "even Solomon in all his glory was not arrayed like one of these."

(Tears streamed down her cheeks as she told how she yearned for those carefree summers at her grand-mother's country cottage). She told how she laid the tear-stained letter aside, when another paper fell from the envelope... a deed to the shop! And there was a paid receipt for a shipment due to arrive within the week! She was blessed... thanks to a messenger of God ...NAJ. To God be the glory!

One by one, the speakers formed a line to tell how God moved in their lives through the obedience of NAJ. But Hugh still had unanswered questions. As the line began to dwindle, the hours ticked away. But Hugh had a sense that there was a link that had not yet been discovered.

He returned to the microphone to speak to the congregation. He looked at the faces of the men and women whose lives were changed because a man took God's word and planned his days accordingly. Hugh knew his words had to be prayerfully presented.

He looked across the sanctuary. Jasmine and her triplets were smiling. Paul was beaming... (he and Jas-mine were expecting a baby in May). John and Olivia were holding hands. Bethany and Jacob came with the scoutmaster, Ben, who asked Bethany to marry him on

Christmas day.

The Pearson family sat on the third row. Alan had his arm around Natalie, not caring if the whole world saw how much he loved her. Of course, George and Dorothy sat next to them but something sparkling caught the pastor's eye. As George squeezed Dorothy's hand, he noticed the engagement ring she wore with pride.

Edie Henson sat on the front row with her new family, *Aunt* Eleanor and *Uncle* Elmer. Edie wanted to make sure they were up front so they could hear the service clearly.

Frank Leacock and his wife Emily were seated behind the Pearsons. They were the proud parents of five sons! And as Frank would say, "They're all boys!" Hugh knew just what that meant. The boys were full of energy and mischief, but Frank knew just how to calm them down. It helped that the ex-sheriff, Mitch Randolph sold him the cabin at Warden Lake.

Emily said cabins were supposed to have only one or two bedrooms but Mitch's cabin had four bedrooms and a den! She wasn't complaining, though. The den, she said, would make a lovely nursery for her little baby girl. She quickly assured her stunned husband that she was only wishing.

Hank and Corene Dudley sat close to the back door. He started coming to church pretty often, but he was still wondering if the roof would hold up under the shock of his attendance. Corene didn't care where they sat as long as they were together.

Seated next to Hank and Corene was Rick and Linda Sharp. Rick was a sub-contractor who lost his job a few years ago. His home was in foreclosure, his truck was repossessed and soon he gave up. He just walked away from his wife, believing he had no life to offer her.

Linda moved back with her parents; and Rick disappeared. But he was given a chance to get back some self respect. When he was finished with the job at Corene's Bed and Breakfast Inn, the jobs were coming in so quickly, he soon had to hire help. That was when he called his wife to join him. Corene and Hank gave them a room at the inn while they were building their own home. They plan to be moving in *before the baby* arrives. Rick will never forget the day he approached that 1985 Lincoln Town Car to ask for a handout. Instead, he got the hand of God, lifting him out of his prison of hopelessness and despair. It was his answered prayer. Corene and Hank became like family. She led him in the sinner's prayer and God gave him a new life.

Daryl and Nicole sat in the last pew on the right side of the sanctuary (closest to the restrooms). Tuyen and Thien visited the restrooms often. Nicole believes they are amazed by the things most Americans take for granted, like flushing toilets and ice makers. (In their Rose Creek home, someone keeps using all the ice cubes and one little angel's hands are always very cold).

Hugh saw Daryl drive into the churchyard in the 1985 Lincoln Town Car and when Nicole followed in close behind, he knew there had to be an explanation. After the service, he would ask Daryl about the car.

As another speaker reached the podium, the man next in line turned pale. Hugh tried to reach him to support him but the man's legs began to tremble and he was helped into a nearby chair. Those in the pews began to whisper loudly and the pastor rushed to the front of the church. There was a hush that fell over the crowd as all eyes focused on the back doors of the church.

Martin Burdine had entered the church, an act he swore he would never do. He wanted nothing to do with Christianity. He disliked any talk of Jesus Christ or His church. Whenever a form requested religious affiliation, he listed 'Atheism.' All of Forest Hills was aware of this fact...and yet here he was now approaching the microphone at the podium!

He stepped up to the platform and touched the man who was helped to a chair. "Is it really you?"

Martin lifted the man's head and stared into the eyes of his son, Stephen, who he had not seen since 1985. "Son, is it really you?" The younger man reached for his father and held him close. For just a moment, the two shared their joy, tears washing away the years of bitterness and pain.

Martin Burdine helped his son to his feet and together they approached the microphone. "Please accept my apology for this interruption of your service. I owe all of you an explanation." He took his handkerchief and wiped his eyes. "You see, this is my son, Stephen." His voice cracked with emotion. "I have not seen my son in more than twenty years..." Trying hard to maintain his composure, he clutched at his son's jacket, pulling him close. "I have been a fool."

Stephen Burdine was still recovering from the idea of seeing his father walk through the doors of the church. But he swallowed hard and managed to say, "No, Dad, I think you were just blindsided..." He saw the confusion in the crowd and hurried to say, "I am Stephen Burdine and this is my father, Martin. We do, indeed, owe all of you an explanation.

Pastor, ould it be all right if we take up some of your service... if you don't mind... and we may be able to answer some of your questions." Hugh encouraged them to speak, "But are you sure you wouldn't be more comfortable in a more private setting? My office is open, if you'd like."

Martin replied, "No, I think it's time for Forest Hills to hear our story, if you don't mind." Hugh answered, "No, by all means, take all the time you need, please."

The two men stood face to face and still felt the shock of their meeting after all the years they were apart. With a smile, Stephen motioned to his father to speak at the microphone.

"In the summer of 1946, I lost my wife, Delia. We were about to be parents and we were in the hospital when her water broke and she went into labor. But she had a heart condition we were not aware of." He paused and cleared his throat. "She wasn't strong enough to go through the labor process." His voice was hoarse as he relived the days of his anguish. "She knew she was dying but she lived long enough to give our son his name, 'Stephen James Burdine.' Then she made me promise to love him enough for both of us." He broke down and cried a few heartfelt tears. "But I let her down..."

Stephen touched his father's arm and said, "No, Dad. You never let her down." Martin continued, "We were quite a team, Stephen and Dad. We fished and camped out and went to ballgames... all the things we men like to call 'living the good life.' I was so proud of my boy..." He looked at Stephen and said, "I still am." Then he turned to the congregation.

"When Stephen graduated from high school with honors, colleges and universities lined up for a chance to enroll my son. I was proud to say he was accepted at Harvard and majored in business. He took classes in economics and I knew one day my son would be a successful businessman. Delia would be so proud of her son and of me for educating him!" He glanced at his son.

"After Stephen graduated, he went into sales. He opened and operated one of the most successful Ford franchises in the industry. His motto was 'When you want the best... Burdine beats the rest.' A small metal tag was affixed to each vehicle that read, 'A Burdine Best.' And Stephen Burdine was the best dealer in all three states!"

He paused and said, "But once you've reached the pinnacle, where do you go from there? I have to say, I worried that there weren't too many career moves available to him. He was making more money than I was and I was a physician! But when he made the decision to change careers, it broke my heart!"

Stephen hugged his father and waited until the older man was seated comfortably. He picked up the microphone and said, "I hadn't planned on making any major changes in my career but sometimes we

don't know what's around the corner. I know I sure
didn't. As Dad said, I was very successful. I made
good money and even though I had no wife or child,
I figured some day I would settle down and meet the
woman of my dreams. But the person who changed
my life was not my future wife.

One day I was hustling my sales department to
top the record breaking month with even more sales
than we ever made before. I had all of them rushing
around and I was feeling the static in the air from all
the high pressure frenzy... and I shouted out to them...
'What day is this?' I expected someone to come back
with, 'this is the day I topped the sales!' But instead
I heard one man say, "This is the day the Lord has
made; Let us rejoice and be glad in it!"

I stopped and it seemed as though time itself had
stopped. I looked around to see where the words had
originated! There was something surreal in that voice!
Then I saw him... Neimann Jackson. Then..." Stephen
smiled and pointed toward heaven, "I saw Him...Jesus
Christ." I never saw the man Jesus Christ but in that
little old man from Malta... in his spirit, I saw the very
heart of Jesus Christ. I asked the man into my office
... and within moments, I invited Jesus Christ into my
heart. My life was never the same."

Martin stood to his feet and came back to the
podium. "That night Stephen told me he got saved
and I asked him, 'saved from what?' He started to
tell me about this Jesus and I got angry. He wanted
to spend the rest of his life worshipping an unseen
God! And claimed that Jesus Christ was His son. I
was so furious with the man who walked into Burdine
Ford and walked away with his heart!

I was determined Stephen would not become a
religious man. I had vowed that the night my Delia
crossed over into death. I prayed to God to save her
life but either He chose not to save her or there was
no God to hear my cries. That was when I vowed He
could not have my son. And now a follower of Jesus
Christ walked into our camp and took my son away.

I told Stephen I would not permit it. If he chose this Jesus over his own father, then he was no longer my son. I disowned him. And he chose Jesus Christ over me. My heart was broken. I waited for him to change his mind. But we never spoke after that day. And one day, I drove by the dealership and the sign was being taken down. I stopped and asked what was happening?"

Stephen came back to the microphone. "After my father gave me that ultimatum, I fasted and prayed. Mr. Jackson told me certain important answers from God required prayer and fasting and he taught me so many things in the next few weeks that followed. So when I received my answer, I also received my own calling. I sold my business quickly and gave my life to the service of my Lord and King, Jesus Christ. I became a missionary in South America."

Martin stood beside his son and added, "We lost contact. I moved to Forest Hills and I had no idea of my son's whereabouts. I was adamant more than ever that I was an atheist. Not only did this so-called God not save my wife but now He claimed my only son! And to make matters worse, I have been haunted by Stephen's automobile. It's come to Forest Hills and I still haven't solved the mystery."

Stephen laughed. "It is no mystery, Dad. When I made up my mind to go into the mission field, I had no use for my expensive 1985 Lincoln Town Car. It had a privacy window installed and even a buzzer to tell the driver I wanted his attention. What use would I have for such an expensive vehicle in a land where there were no highways? So I gave it to my mentor, Neimann Jackson. He was getting up in years and I couldn't imagine a better ride for him."

Pastor Hayden was excited to hear the answer to his riddle of the Town Car. He stepped up to the microphone. "Stephen you are a walking miracle. Do you have time to stay around and tell our people more about your life's work as a missionary? We could schedule you at your convenience, of course."

Stephen agreed. "I'd like that and I'll have time to spend with my father too. We have a lot of years of catching up to do." Martin was overjoyed.

"Stephen, there's one more thing I need to tell you. I've professed for years to be an atheist. But I have to tell you, after seeing your Town Car so often, I had hoped you were here looking for me. But I as still too hard-hearted to change. Then when Mr... I mean Pastor Hayden told me about this memorial, I told him I would not come. But something was still drawing me here. I drove by and saw your Lincoln and I spoke to this God of yours. I said, 'If this is what it takes to find my son once more, then You truly are God. And I intend to learn of You.' And Stephen, my son, since He brought you to my front door, you need to introduce me to Jesus, Son."

The old man looked into the eyes of his son and saw the embodiment of answered prayers. He shook the hand of his son, and his son held tightly to his father's hand... both Fathers' hands.

The candles were glowing as the evening progressed. The New Year was approaching and the pastor led them in praise and worship. Stephen Burdine led the people in the hymn, 'Rock of Ages.' Martin had no idea his son had such a beautiful tenor voice.

But as the song changed to 'Just As I Am,' the words began to soften the old man's heart...('Just as I am, without one plea, but that Thy blood was shed for me, and that Thou biddst me come to Thee, O Lamb of God, I come! I come!')

Martin Burdine became the newest Christian in Forest Hills as he knelt at the altar with his son, Stephen, who led him in the sinner's prayer. Hugh remembered saying miracles were in season! He was still glowing from the spiritual highlights of the night when he stepped into his office. The last guest walked out into the parking lot and Hugh noticed Daryl had left the Lincoln and rode home with Nicole. Some issues were still unresolved. But as he turned on his desk light, he saw an envelope... with gold angel wings and silver letters...NAJ.

Opening the envelope, Hugh found a letter in script, *'To every thing there is a season, and a time to every purpose under the heaven: A time to be born, and a time to die; A time to plant, and a time to pluck up that which is planted; A time to kill, and a time to heal; A time to break down, and a time to build up; A time to weep, and a time to laugh; A time to mourn, and a time to dance; A time to cast away stones, and a time to gather stones together; A time to embrace, and a time to refrain from embracing; A time to get, and a time to lose: A time to keep, and a time to cast away; A time to rend, and a time to sew; A time to keep silence, and a time to speak.'*

The time has come to bring peace to Forest Hills for God is not a creator of confusion. I leave my Last Will and Testament in your capable hands; I ask that you would be the Executor of my will, aiding those in God's kingdom with wisdom and faith. In my Father's service, I have placed your name as the sole beneficiary of NAJ Executive Accounts, with only one request.

It is my one desire that you would oversee the transfer of the title and documents of my beautiful 1985 Lincoln Town Car to Daryl Baker.

The privacy vault in the rear passenger section also holds legal documents to the real estate located on Backbone Mountain, consisting of twenty acres and the four bedroom, 2250 sq. ft. house which are to be given to Daryl for his years of faithful service. Daryl's birthplace will be a good place to raise his daughters.

It has been a magnificent journey, Pastor Hugh Hayden. Your father is very proud of your life's work, as am I. And now I wait to meet you again...at our Father's table... Signed, NAJ.

Hugh pulled back the curtain, looking out at the Lincoln Town Car. 'What an amazing journey one man can take with a willing spirit and an open heart' ...men like Neimann Jackson and Michael Genucci.

EPILOGUE

The clinic was empty now. Two young men had been taken to the morgue. The twelve year old boy ingested his older brother's drugs. He was pronounced dead on arrival. The older brother would have been twenty next month, but his guilt consumed him.

He stepped outside the clinic doors and slowly opened the toolbox of his truck. Then he stepped into eternity. A self inflicted gunshot wound ended his life. Two senseless deaths and the mother is screaming out to God. Where do they go from here?

An envelope is traveling to Canton, Ohio by a special carrier. It has the feel of currency and in the upper left-hand corner is the scale of justice in gold with two silver letters ... M.G.

THE ... END?

About the author:

Photo by Michelle Jones

     Helen Hill lives in Lake City, Florida with her husband, Danny, (the owner/ operator of 'Danny's Auto and Truck Repair') and her pampered pet poodle, 'Baby Girl,' who owns everything else!

     Helen has been writing fiction stories since 1972. This is Helen's second book. Her first work was "Searching for Holy Ground," published in 2009.

     Helen and Danny are actively involved in their home church, First Full Gospel Church in Lake City, Florida. The Hills love to share the remarkable miracles God has given them so freely and is quick to offer prayer to anyone at anytime!

     May Manny's Gift be a blessing to you!

Made in the USA
Charleston, SC
19 September 2014